Monster

By Nikki Reiter

Twelve

I don't want to do this anymore. I feel like a corpse, rotting, dead. I am not living. He made sure of that. I am hanging on by a single decaying thread. I don't want to continue like this anymore. Feeling dead. I am trapped in this darkness. It doesn't have a future. All I can do is enter a dream and pray that I will never wake up.

I no longer exist to the outside world.

He has me here. Trapped in the darkness, alone and isolated.

I don't know where here is. I wish I could say, but I don't know. I don't know how long I've been here. It feels like years, but it could be months, maybe even weeks. I don't know.

He has robbed me of everything, including my name. I never thought that was possible. He calls me Twelve. I don't know if that is my actual name. I don't think it is. Right now, I just can't remember.

That's the only thing he calls me, Twelve, with his icy, cold voice. It sends chills down my spine. Every time he speaks it. Twelve.

Twelve. That is not my name! It can't be!

It can't be.

I am not Twelve.

Instead, I call myself Mandy.

I don't know if that is my actual name. Maybe it's some made-up memory. Mandy. I dwell on that name, and it makes me feel human. I was born human, at least I think I was, but now I am a scared animal locked up in a cage.

My life is trivial. Nothing about me matters. He's made sure of that. I don't matter, not to him. Not to the outside word. He is the only one that exists.

I can see his deranged, maniacal look. It is embedded in the darkness. It is the only thing that I can see. I lie here, cold and naked, on a hard cement floor. My hands and feet are tied. I have duct tape over my eyes.

I can feel him in me. I can taste him on my lips. My stomach churns as I repress the urge to vomit. I feel sick and filthy.

I just want it to end. I fantasize about chomping down on my tongue. I wonder how long it would take to bleed out.

I don't do it.

I can't.

I keep going. I don't know how I have the energy to keep going, but I do. I can't fight back. I won't. I won't give him the satisfaction that he's broken me, dehumanized me, made into this filthy pathetic shell. I just lie here, too weak and too tired.

I don't have any warmth left inside of me. I feel like I have freezing-cold water running through my veins. I want him to kill me. Why doesn't he just end it and get it over with? Even when he is not around, I can feel his hands wrapped around my throat, squelching the life out of me. He holds me captive in the darkness. I can't break free from his grip. He is too strong. I'm gasping for air, but there is none.

I haven't slept for ages. I tremble at every sound. He tries to break me. I won't let him. I can't.

Twelve. Every time he calls me that, I shout out, "Mandy! My name is Mandy!"

My name is Mandy. Even if it is not, it definitely isn't Twelve.

My name is Mandy. I repeat it to myself. If I can just will myself to believe that my name is Mandy and not Twelve, he won't win.

I spend my days thinking about my family. I miss them so much. I think about my parents. I can't even begin to imagine how hard this must be for them.

I wonder if they are still out there looking for me. Or did they just give up? I like to think they are looking. It's hard for me to imagine, though. It's hard for me to imagine anything outside of this room.

In the back of my mind, in the darkness, lingers the ultimate question: will my family ever see me again? If so, will I be alive, or will it be in a morgue? I try not to think like that. I try to be optimistic. How can one be optimistic, living in hell?

I try to make sense of everything.

It was a beautiful, sunny spring day. The sky was the most fantastic shade of blue that I have ever seen in my life.

The sun was bright. It was warming everything up from the inside out. It felt nice, especially after the harsh winter.

I wonder if that day was really magnificent or if it's a figment of my imagination, a glimmer of hope. Hope that maybe I will be able to see the sun again. Does it still exist? I wonder…

It was a fantastic day outside. I decided to go for a walk. I always did before I went to work. I just loved being outside. I was a video game designer. I always seemed to be holed up in the office. My coworkers described me as being a workaholic. Sometimes, I would forget that there even was a world out there.

That day, when I was getting ready for my walk, something told me not to go. As always, I ignored my instincts. I thought I was being paranoid from all the scary movies I watched the night before.

That morning, when I opened my curtains, I saw a black Nissan with tinted windows. It was parked in front of my neighbor's house. Suddenly, my heart sank into the pit of my stomach. The hairs on the back of my neck stood on end. For some unexplainable reason, I had a bad feeling, the worst that I'd ever had in my life. It was an irrational feeling.

I lived in a small, close-knit, middle-class community. Everybody there knew everybody else. That Nissan caught my attention because I knew all the cars. I knew who drove what and what belonged to whom. Nobody in my community owned a Nissan. It stuck out like a sore thumb.

I sat on the couch, staring out the window. I felt as if somebody was staring back at me.

"Get a grip," I said to myself. "That's the last time I let Jason talk me into binge-watching horror flicks." My brother and I had done a twenty-four-hour scary movie marathon the day before.

I put my sneakers on and went outside. It was a beautiful day. I wanted to enjoy the outdoors as much as possible before going to work. I wasn't going to deny myself my daily walk because the scary movies had me on edge.

The moment my foot hit the pavement, my heart sank into the pit of my stomach. I had that really bad feeling again. My instincts told me to go inside and lock the doors, but I told myself the fear was irrational, and I ignored it.

I walked up the sidewalk. That's when I saw the Nissan. For a moment, it was keeping my pace. It was eerie. My heart was pounding so hard it felt like it was going to explode. The palms of my hands became cold and sweaty. The Nissan finally drove off down the road.

I thought I was being paranoid from those movies I'd watched with Jason. After all, I lived in an awesome community, one where you didn't need to lock your doors. Nothing ever happened there. Some would find it quite boring, but I found it charming.

I was a mile away from the house, enjoying the weather, when I saw that same black Nissan. I felt panicky. My instincts told me to run and to put as much distance between the car and myself as possible.

I ignored my instincts and kept walking. I was debating with myself if I should tell Jason about this. The movie marathon had me really on edge. I could just imagine what Jason would say…

The car drove slowly by again. I felt like prey being stalked by a predator.

"There is no reason to worry," I said to myself. "I just have to lay off the horror movies for a while." I continued on, enjoying the weather.

A few blocks later, I was crossing the street when I saw that same black Nissan parked in a no-parking zone. The engine was on. The passenger-side window was open slightly. I could see puffs of cigarette smoke escaping the car. I had the impression that it was waiting for me.

Monster

I found her. Number twelve. From now on, that will be her new name. Her regular name will no longer exist. Names should be used for people. Not objects. She is an object. She will come to know me as Lord.

That is my name. I am the evolution of mankind. I am better than your regular person. I am much better than that. I am Lord.

She will be mine.

Twelve.

I first discovered her six months ago. It was in the fall. I was driving around aimlessly, bored. I remember that day clearly. The air was chilled. It was very windy. There was a slight rain. It was more like a mist. According to the squirrels and other wildlife, it was going to be a very cold winter.

It was like magic. I was just driving around. Then there she was. Poof! Just like that. She was something from my dreams.

And there she was, walking along the sidewalk. The coldness and wetness didn't seem to bother her any. She just strolled along, her head up.

I could feel her confidence radiating off her with every stride. I found that alluring. I wanted her. God, did I ever.

At that moment, I knew she was mine. I wanted her to join my collection. I needed her to.

She was different from the others. The others were timid and shy. They lacked confidence. At first, I sought out women whose confidence and self-esteem were shattered. I'm not ashamed to admit it, but when I first started this game, I didn't have any confidence in myself. With each object, my confidence grew.

But the excitement that I'd felt with the others was no longer there. I didn't even realize it until that day. I was on the prowl for something different. I wanted something more, something exciting and challenging.

There she was, the exact opposite of the eleven others. That just made her more desirable.

I watched her for months. I learned everything about her and her family. I studied her routine inside and out. I knew her.

She was a video game designer. I even said hi to her one day. It was right in front of where she worked. She just blew me off. She did most people. She thought she was better than everybody else. The worst part was that she didn't even realize it.

She was full of herself, hardheaded, and stubborn. When I learned that about her, I wasn't sure if I would like it, but I was up to the challenge. There was just something about her. I yearned for her.

She loved to walk. She would walk the same path every morning before going to work. Rain or shine, it didn't matter. She would always be out there walking. She would leave her house at the same time every day. Nine o'clock on the dot. You could set your watch by her. In fact, I did set my watch by her.

She would leave her house at nine, walk three miles, and then turn around and walk another three miles back to her house. She walked the same route every day, never varying her routine. Once home, she would take a shower. The shower always lasted ten minutes. An hour later, she would leave for work.

She never locked her doors. Nobody in her neighborhood did. They didn't have to. It was a scene from Mr. Rogers' Neighborhood. It was sickening.

It normally took her fifteen minutes to get to work, ten if there wasn't any traffic. I would always wait ten minutes after she left before I strolled right into her house.

It was a beautiful house too. It was something that no twenty-two-year-old should be able to afford. It was a split-level, with two bedrooms and two full baths.

I would take a shower in her shower. I would nap on her bed. I would rummage through her closet and dresser. I rummaged through her belongings. Her family and her work were her life. I wanted, I needed, to know everything about her. I wanted to know more about her than she knew about herself. In those months, I got to know her intimately well.

She was a very young soul, very young, very successful, and very arrogant. She lived in a perfect world, sheltered from life. That had to change.

She really wasn't like the others. She was tall, athletic, and beautiful. She had so much confidence and so much pride. It was nauseating.

Where the others were weak, she was strong. Radiant. Irresistible.

***

Spring is the rebirth of everything, so that is when I decided that I would take her. It was the first day of spring. It was a beautiful day too. The sun glowed perfection in the brilliant blue sky.

I couldn't wait for her to join my collection.

The day before, I'd rented a black Nissan. I parked it in front of the house across the street from hers. I watched her as she moved around in her house. She was so graceful. Everything seemed to come so easily to her. It wasn't fair.

The anticipation was killing me. I couldn't wait for her to become mine. Her confidence gave me confidence. God, I'd never felt like that before, almost giddy. For a while, I felt like the king of the world. She would be number twelve. That would be her new name. I will make sure of that. She will forget her name. After all, she was an object and didn't deserve an actual name. I couldn't wait for her to be mine. The thought excited me.

I took smoke out of my jacket pocket, cracked open the window on the driver's side, and lit a cigarette, savoring the taste of it. My other hand drummed against the steering wheel.

I don't know why people insist on giving women names. That should be a privilege. After all, women are not people. They are nothing more than objects. Twelve wasn't really a name anyway. It was a designation, a way for me to distinguish her from the others.

Twelve left her house at nine in the morning that day. The second she stepped out of her house, she stared at the Nissan, wondering whose car it could have been. I could see the confusion in her eyes. For a split second, I feared that she would go back inside. She walked cautiously across her front porch. Slowly, she walked down the steps, her eyes never leaving my car. A moment later, she dismissed the car and began her daily jaunt.

I followed her. I would drive past her, turn at the intersection, and then, a few seconds later, I would once again be behind her. It was all a game. Women are the game pieces. I was toying with her. I wanted her to know. It was more like I needed her to know that there were things to fear. After all, she lived in a great neighborhood. Crime didn't seem to exist there. Nobody in her community locked their doors at night or when they went out. They didn't have to, and that needed to change.

Women should not be allowed to live in nice areas. They don't deserve it, especially when so many people are homeless or living in slums.

Women are just objects. Nothing more.

It used to bother me growing up. I always lived in the crappiest parts of town with my mother. She was a crack whore. I never knew my father. I don't think she even knew who my father was. My mother would always take me with her when she met up with her johns. Or she would bring them over to our place, selling herself for crack cocaine.

I was sitting in the Nissan, staring off into space, reminiscing about the past. Twelve slowed down when she saw me. She started walking at a snail's pace. There was uncertainty in her eyes.

Good.

It was starting to work.

I stared at her, undressing her with my eyes, imagining all the things I could do to her. I wanted her. God, did I ever. I wanted to take her right then. Instead, I waited. She was feeling uneasy. I wanted her to feel vulnerable, helpless even.

I wanted to take her. I waited, though. It took all my willpower, but the timing had to be perfect. There is an entire ritual that I have down. I have to follow it. It makes the experience that much more gratifying.

I waited.

I planned on taking her in front of her house. That way, safety would be within arm's reach, but no, it would never come. The experience would be that much more terrifying for her. My stomach fluttered with excitement. I can't wait until she is all mine. I felt like a little kid at Christmas time. I'd never felt like that with the others. It was a great feeling of euphoric bliss.

She will call me Lord. The other eleven objects did. I deserve it. After all, I am almighty and powerful. I make sure these objects know it. Snatching her right in front of her own home in the middle of the day would prove to her just how powerful I am.

I drove off. In the rearview mirror, I could see a sense of relief in Twelve's eyes. That's part of the ritual, giving the object a small sense of peace.

I didn't have to be there for her entire jaunt. I just wanted to make my presence known. I love making my prey sweat before jumping in to make the kill. It's all a part of the game.

I pulled the car up to the sidewalk and parked the car. The engine was still on. I moved over to the passenger seat. I opened the window a crack and lit a cigarette.

I waited. My heart was racing. A few minutes later, Twelve appeared from around the corner. When she did, I put out my cigarette.

Twelve

I don't remember what happened next. Everything happened so quickly. I ended up lying on the sidewalk, my head bouncing off the cement, and I started to feel lightheaded. My vision blurred.

I saw a man with wild, dark hair and dark eyes lying on top of me. He reeked of stale cigarettes, cologne, and gin.

"Come on. Fight back. Yell for help." His hand covered my mouth as he spoke to me. His voice reminded me of ice. There was urgency or a need in his voice. At the same time, he was calm.

I couldn't scream for help. I tried. I couldn't breathe. His knee was resting on my diaphragm. My ribs felt like they would be crushed under the man's weight. He was holding both of my hands over my head with his one hand. I could feel my wrists bruising underneath his tight grasp. His other hand was struggling for a roll of duct tape.

The last thing I remember was that horrible, demented look. It is a look that is sketched in the darkness of my mind. I couldn't fight him off. I didn't even try, not really. I couldn't. My head was pulsating. Blood obscured my vision. I passed out.

When I came around, I was lying on a cold cement floor. I still had duct tape over my eyes. Some type of wire bound my hands and feet together. I couldn't move. Every time I did, the restraints became tighter and tighter.

My body ached. My head throbbed. I could feel my hair was matted with blood. I felt nauseous. The room reeked, mostly of urine and feces.

I started to cry out in frustration. I was so upset and confused. I was upset for letting myself get into this situation. If only I'd listened to my instincts, I wouldn't have been there. I knew something wasn't right when I first saw that Nissan. Nothing about it felt right. I was stupid and ignored my gut. It was sitting outside of the house before I left. Everything that was happening was my fault. It was something that I could have prevented. I should have listened to myself. And I didn't.

I was confused because I didn't know what was going on. My brain ended up shutting down. All I knew was that, one moment, I was out enjoying a beautiful day and the next moment, I was here, tied up and covered in blood.

My eyes started to well up with tears. I tried not to cry. I didn't want to show any type of weakness. I couldn't help it. I started sobbing out in frustration. Suddenly, I felt very small and powerless as the situation started to sink in.

Again, I fought against the restraints, not caring that the wire was digging into my skin, cutting off the circulation. I just wanted to get the hell out of there.

In the abyss of everything, I heard a sound. I jumped, my breath catching in my throat. I was suddenly aware that I was not alone. The man was somewhere in the room. I could hear him breathing. I wigged out even more. The more I struggled, the more rapid his breathing became. As soon as

I realized this, I stopped struggling. I stopped moving. I held my breath, listening, waiting.

I don't think I have ever been so terrified in my life as I was in those several minutes when I first woke up in the room. Reality, everything, finally caught up to me. I didn't know what to do or even how I was supposed to react. I was scared; for all I knew, he could have been sitting there with a gun to my head. The worst part was I just didn't know. I had no idea what to expect.

Silence filled the room.

Dead silence. It lasted for minutes, maybe even hours. I don't know.

From the other side of the room, I heard a chair moan as the man got up. He made his way toward me. I was counting his steps: one, two, three…nine, ten. I felt his hot, rancid breath on my face. He gently caressed my lips.

I flinched at his every touch. Tears streamed down my face. He untied my feet.

"Good. Now, get up," he whispered. I could feel his lips touching my ear as he spoke. His voice was quiet, calm, but cold and calculating.

He hoisted me to my feet. He pressed his body up against mine, sandwiching me between him and the wall. I started to shake uncontrollably.

"That's a good girl. Now, scream for me."

I didn't. I was too afraid.

He pushed me to the ground. I landed on a mattress. He made sure he was on top of me the entire time. He untied my wrists, holding them above my head with one hand. I could feel blood trickling down my arms. He forced his tongue inside my mouth while thrusting up against me.

My stomach churned. I wanted to vomit.

I couldn't. I couldn't move, paralyzed with fear. I could feel his other hand groping me. He eventually grabbed my shirt and ripped it off. He started to kiss me around my neck and chest.

"Come on. Let me hear you scream," he whispered into my ear. I could feel him undoing my jeans.

"Come on. Let me hear you scream," he said again, thrusting himself harder and harder against me. He still held my hands over my head. He would grab my throat with his other hand, squeezing until I felt like I was going to black out before letting go.

"Let me hear you scream," he repeated again, biting down hard on my nipple.

I was in so much pain. I couldn't move. I couldn't breathe. The only thing I could do was lie there and try not to cry as he kept repeating, "Let me hear you scream." He would then squeeze my neck again until I thought my eyes would pop out.

"Let me hear you scream," he said again, biting down hard on my breast, drawing blood.

I felt horribly filthy. I just lay there. I refused to scream. I didn't fight back. This seemed to infuriate him. I'm not sure what enraged him more, not screaming or not fighting back.

"Fine, I will make you scream," he said coarsely as he got off me.

For a brief second, the thought of escape crossed my mind. He was finally off me. My hands and feet were untied.

As quickly as that thought popped into my head, he was on top of me again. He forced his tongue back into my mouth. He held onto something hard and cold. I don't know what it was. I couldn't see it, but he started to rape me with it.

The entire time he was raping me with the object, he was whispering to me. He was telling me to scream. He wanted me to. He was telling me to fight back. He needed me to. I couldn't. I was too scared. I didn't. I didn't want to give him the satisfaction. Eventually, what seemed like hours later, he stopped raping me with the object.

He tied my hands back together. I must have passed out again. When I woke, I was lying on the hard, cold cement floor. I was lying on my stomach with my hands tied in front of me. I could feel the blood between my legs. I started to cry silent tears. I was afraid that the man was there. I didn't want to do anything that would excite him.

He wasn't in the room. I'm not sure how long it was before I realized that. I was just glad that I was able to breathe again. I stopped holding my breath.

I started to breathe in blood and vomit. I felt like I was drowning in it. I forced myself to roll over to my side to get my face out of the puddle. My body protested the entire time I moved. Every bone in my body ached. After a while, I realized I was still naked. I started to cry even harder.

I didn't sleep that night. I was shivering uncontrollably. I could feel the coldness of the concrete seeping through my skin. My head throbbed, and tears streaked down my face.

I started yelling at myself for being weak.

I wanted nothing more than to wake up from this horrid nightmare. I just wanted to go home. I wanted to be where it was safe and warm. I thought about Jason. He has the most beautiful voice and can play any instrument. He is a musical prodigy. In high school, he started a band, the Free Spirits, and that was what he was, a free spirit. Anytime any of us felt scared, he would sing. He used to joke about it, scaring the monsters away. I tried thinking of one of his songs. I can't remember any of them now. Thinking about him made me think of home; it made me think of the rest of my family. The thought of my family made me vomit as the realization sank in: chances are they would never see me alive again.

Monster

Twelve walked toward the Nissan. She slowed her pace as she cautiously passed the car. She squinted her eyes, trying to see me through the tinted glass.

I locked my eyes with hers. She was tense. Her eyes were wide with fear. I smiled. It felt like we had a connection. At that moment, she knew. The timing was perfect. I waited for the moment her back was toward the car before leaping out and pouncing on her.

She fell forward, hitting her head hard against the sidewalk. She looked dazed and confused. I knelt on top of her, pressing my knee into her diaphragm, dropping my weight. I was able to hold both her hands over her head with my left hand. I had my right hand cupped over her nose and mouth.

"Come on. Fight back. Yell for help," I whispered into her ear. I wanted her to scream for me. I needed her to.

She didn't yell out for help. She didn't even fight back. I don't think she could. I think she was in too much shock.

Blood started to matt her hair. It made her look even more beautiful. Like an angel. I'd known she was going to be different from the others; I just hadn't realized how. By this point, the others had all fought back. They would always do what I told them to, and I would quickly lose interest in them. The game would get boring.

Twelve didn't fight back. She didn't yell for help. Already, she was showing her defiance. I liked that. At the same time, I found that quality annoying.

When I'd first seen Twelve, I'd known she would be mine. It was love at first sight. I did have some doubts about collecting her. I was attracted to her, but she was different from the others. She wasn't my type. That's what made her exotic. She was a fighter in her own way. Because of that, she wasn't playing by the rules.

It was going to be difficult to break her – I knew that from the get-go—but, oh, the possibility. I was looking forward to that. I could start getting creative again. It had been a while. I got into my comfort zone.

Twelve blacked out.

I slowly moved my hand away from her mouth. I made sure that my index finger got caught on her bottom lip. I continued moving my hand down to her throat, grabbing it. I could feel her heart pulsating with my thumb and index finger. I felt even more powerful than I already am.

It was tempting to end the game right then. Not nearly as fun, though. I moved my hand down to her chest, feeling each breast.

I reached into my jacket pocket and took out a roll of duct tape. I tied her hands together. She was conscious for a bit. The fear in her eyes was intoxicating. She drifted back out of consciousness.

I put tape over her mouth. I used the rest of the roll to wrap around her head, covering her eyes. I just kept wrapping it around her head. I wanted to make sure that she couldn't see anything.

I picked her up and put her in the passenger seat of the Nissan. I slipped into the driver's seat and drove off. I wondered if I had any wire left at the house to bind her hands and feet with. I liked using wire better.

***

It was a long drive back to the house. It isn't my house; I inherited it, in a sense. The house originally belonged to John Smith. He doesn't need it anymore. He hasn't needed it for a long while.

I've been thinking about him a lot lately. I owe him. I owe him a lot, actually. I keep all my objects in his basement. It's easier that way.

I don't think he would mind. It's better than letting the place go to waste.

I'd known John since I was a little kid. He was one of my mother's regulars. He was also the one who kept her hooked on coke. As a kid, I probably spent more time at his house than I did at school.

When I was little, I never understood him. He would use women for his own satisfaction. He would beat these women senseless if they didn't comply with what he wanted or needed. He wanted his women to be one hundred percent submissive to him in every way imaginable. He loved using these women as his personal punching bag.

It bugged the hell out of me when I was a kid. I hated seeing this happen. What I never understood was why these women kept coming back for more. Then I figured out a long time ago that women enjoyed it when someone treated them like garbage. I saw the bruises and abrasions that he caused. I saw the broken bones and all the trips to the emergency room. These women, they kept coming back to him. They didn't care.

Why would they? They weren't human. That was my conclusion. No human being would ever want somebody to treat them like that. Women are not people. They never have been. For whatever reason, people have a hard time understanding that.

I did too.

I had just started high school when I saw a senior, the captain of the football team, trying to force a girl into his car. She was crying and telling him to stop. He wouldn't. I jumped in the middle of it. The senior backed down, calling the girl slut and bitch. He went into his car and drove off.

The girl and I talked. It surprised me. She was actually upset with me for hitting her boyfriend. She was making excuses for his behavior. She was back with him a few days later.

There were several other girls at my high school who were in abusive relationships. If I saw a guy hitting a girl, I would always intervene. Yet these girls would be pissed at me.

"Why'd you do that? You had no right to interfere! He wasn't going to hurt me."

That is what they always told me. I didn't get it. Why would anybody want to be used and abused? It didn't make sense. That was something I always asked my mother. She could never answer the question to my satisfaction.

That's when I started to understand. Women aren't people.

My mother understood this. She knew what her role in life was. She would allow men to use and abuse her. She never cared. All her friends understood that. They would allow men to use and abuse them as well.

After college, I moved into a nice apartment building. It was in the same town as John Smith. I didn't even realize it, not consciously, anyway. John lived in a slum part of town, on the wrong side of the tracks. I lived on the other side of the tracks, in the lower-middle-class part of town.

I have never done drugs. I have never been in trouble with the law, not even a speeding ticket. I always treated people with respect, even women. As far as I was concerned, I had nothing in common with John Smith other than my mother. I had run off to college to escape from it all.

It was nothing more than a fluke that I ran into John. It was a little over ten years ago. I was hanging out at a bar in the neighboring town. I had just landed a decent job, six months out of college. Some friends and I were hanging out to celebrate.

I was walking up to the bar when I recognized John right away. He didn't recognize me, of course.

I hadn't seen him since I was a kid. I'll never be able to forget him. I will never forget all the times he sent my mother to the hospital. He would beat her senseless. I would watch helplessly in the corner.

"You are not going back to him, are you?" I would ask my mother every time.

"You're too young to understand. When you're older, you will." That was her response every time.

Anyway, John and I got to talking. I bought him several drinks just to keep him talking. He still lived in his bungalow. His parents had died a few years back, and he'd inherited a huge chunk of change. He had stopped working.

I don't know why, but I kept buying him drinks. I felt compelled to keep him talking. It fascinated me how women would always go to him. He wasn't good-looking or anything. He was cruel. He was not a nice person. Women loved it. Yet I couldn't even get a woman to talk to me.

It surprised me. I actually enjoyed listening to him.

He told me about this teenage girl, Janis. She was crazy for him. He loved it, that a man his age was with a girl who was barely legal. He loved how submissive she was. She was easy to mold. The way John told it, she liked having somebody smack her around.

A few hours later, John left the bar. I stayed until it closed. My friends had left hours earlier. I never even realized it. As I was making my way toward my car, I saw a person slumped over a steering wheel. The car was parked underneath a street lamp. I never would have noticed it if it hadn't been for the light.

I cautiously made my way over to that car. I wanted to make sure that the person was okay. That's when I noticed it was John. His sleeves were rolled up. He had track marks on his arm. The syringe was in his lap.

His car was unlocked. I opened the door to check his pulse. There was no pulse. His heart was not beating. I held my hand over his mouth for a couple of minutes. I couldn't feel his breath on my hand. I'm guessing he died from an overdose.

I don't know why – I wasn't really thinking, just reacting to the situation – but I found John's wallet and took out his driver's license. I wanted to know his address. I moved him over to the passenger side of the car. I slid into the driver's seat. I drove him back home.

I carried him into his house and dragged him down into the basement. I then went out and bought a ton of cat litter. I came back to his house and covered him up with the cat litter, hoping that it would help with the smell of decomposition.

I kept his bungalow, paying all his bills and credit cards. I put his car in the garage, along with most of his stuff. I never went back into that garage. That's his area now, not mine. I respect that.

I didn't know what I was planning on doing with his house. I just knew that I wanted it. I'd never lived in a house before. If somebody like him deserved something like that, why didn't I? I wasn't thinking straight. I just wanted his house. I fixed it up to my liking.

A couple of weeks after John's death, I was hanging out at his house, adding some final finishes to it. I had kept all his furniture. I hadn't brought any of my personal belongings to his house. That felt wrong and disrespectful. I'd scrubbed the place down and repainted it. It was shaggy-looking from the outside. Inside, it had been even worse. I wanted to return it back to its original glory.

I had just finished repairing the shutters on the windows. The outside was finally starting to look nice. I was in the kitchen, grabbing another beer out of the fridge, when a teenage girl came knocking.

She was in her late teens. She was a little taller than five feet and looked like she weighed about seventy pounds soaking wet. She had dark, thin hair. She wore it down in front of her face like curtains. It made her thin face look fuller. She had bad acne and acne scars all over her face.

She wore a blue miniskirt and a matching top. She was a timid, shy girl. She wasn't good-looking, and she knew it. If you could look past all the acne and her thinness, she could have been pretty.

She was very self-conscious.

"Where's John?" Her voice trembled a bit when she spoke. She didn't even look me in the eyes.

"He's not here. He moved out."

"No, he wouldn't have. He loves me too much. He would have told me."

"You know, I think I have his forwarding address. If you want to wait a minute, I can see if I can find it for you. Come inside if you like."

I took a step back into the kitchen, turning my back to her. I walked over to the table, which was littered with all types of papers and documents. I kept the door open. The girl stood there in the doorway, not moving. I assumed this was the girl John had told me about the night at the bar.

John had told me that she'd been the victim of bullying and cruel jokes. The neighborhood kids would tease her relentlessly about her looks. These kids were extremely vicious about it.

One day, the altercation had turned physical, and John had intervened. He had saved the day. John had chatted up the girl, making her feel for the first time important and wanted, even beautiful.

I had known John since I was a little kid. I knew the type of person he was. He was good at looking inside people, especially vulnerable women. He could see their insecurities and use that to his advantage. He was a dog. He would beat the hell out of these women if they didn't do what he wanted sexually, no matter how degrading.

"Janis, is it?" I glanced over my shoulder. The girl nodded. "Yeah, John and I, we're old buddies. He talked about you a bit."

The girl perked up some. She took a step inside the house. She had old bruises all over her arms and some fresh bruises on top of them, courtesy of John, I'm sure.

"Where'd you get the bruises from?"

I don't remember her response. I don't remember what I said after. I wasn't paying any attention. I acted concerned for her well-being. I wanted her to let her guard down. She was starting to feel safe with me.

Good.

"Ah, I found his address," I said after several long minutes of rummaging through papers on the kitchen table and making idle conversation. I handed her a blank piece of paper.

She took the paper. She looked down at the page with confusion in her eyes. She wasn't afraid exactly. She was just confused, uncertain of what was happening.

I touched her cheek.

"You deserve better than this," I told her, indicating the bruises on her arms. I traced my finger down her jaw.

She freaked out. She swatted my hand away as she stepped back, bumping into the wall. She was yelling. I grabbed her elbows.

She yelled even louder. She was trying to fight back. I had her pinned up against the wall. I covered her mouth with my hand, hoping to muffle her screams.

It was arousing, feeling her squirm away from me.

I needed to get her to stop screaming. I didn't want her to alert any of the neighbors. I doubt anybody would have done anything in this neighborhood. Still, I didn't want to take any chances.

"Shh, it's okay. It's okay. I'm not going to hurt you. I swear. That was never my intention. I just. I just don't know what you see in John. First, he's like forty years older than you are. And I know how he treats his women. You don't deserve him. You are better than that. You deserve better." I eased up on her some. I removed my hand from her mouth.

"I'm not going to hurt you. I'm not, but I can't have you screaming at me, okay?"

She nodded. She started to relax some. I let go of her. I was still standing in her space. I just wasn't touching her anymore.

"John didn't really move, did he?" she stuttered out. Her voice sounded small.

"No, he didn't." I took a step back from her. "He's in the basement. He's pretty messed up. He was in a bad car accident not too long ago. He's doped up on some medications. He didn't want any visitors. Anyway, you don't need him. You can do better, but that's not for me to say. You can go down to the basement if you like. I don't think he would mind. Or I can see if he can come up here."

The girl remained where she was.

"It's up to you. And I am truly sorry about any misunderstanding."

To my surprise, she just shook her head. "Stay up here," she said sternly. I was surprised. I didn't think she had it in her. She walked to the basement door. I walked over and closed the kitchen door. I locked it. Once the girl was at the bottom of the stairs, I followed her down.

I hadn't lied to her. John Smith was in the basement.

She turned around when she saw his remains. Mortal terror was etched deeply into her face. It actually made her look beautiful. Next thing I knew, she was lying on the floor, and I was on top of her.

"Please don't. Please don't. Please don't," she kept whimpering.

I hitched up her skirt. She cried the entire time. I don't understand why. She was into guys like John Smith. John was scum. He was trash. He was an evil person. His death was a blessing. His life was a curse to the rest of the community.

I remember everything he did around me. I remember clearly how he treated my mother and the other women.

The girl tried fighting back. She begged me to stop. Her struggles made it more arousing. After a while, she stopped fighting. Instead, she asked me for my name.

"It's Lord. My name is Lord," I whispered into her ear.

"Lord, please stop!" she cried out. It was great hearing her say my name like that.

After I was done, I kissed her on her mouth.

"That was wonderful. The best I ever had. Thank you," I said, getting off her, and then she clobbered me hard across the face. I hadn't been expecting that. I didn't think she had any spunk in her. I was dazed for a moment.

She started screaming as loud as she could. It pissed me off.

She wouldn't stop screaming. It was more like a loud and high-pitched shriek. It was giving me a headache. She was ascending the stairs. I was able to grab her ankle and pull her down the steps.

She rolled over on her back. I straddled her. She was fighting and squirming to get free.

"Everything is going to be okay," I kept promising her.

I had my hands around her neck. I could feel her pulse beating. I could feel her heart pounding throughout her body. It was an invigorating feeling. I had never felt so alive.

She looked like a scared deer trapped in headlights.

"It's going to be okay," I told her again as I snapped her neck. The beating stopped. It was the most arousing type of high I'd ever experienced. I fell in love with having complete power over another. It made me feel powerful and alive for the first time. It was almost nirvana.

To this day, she is still in the basement. All eleven objects are. Their bones adorn the walls and floor. It's a safe place where I keep my women.

***

I pulled into the driveway of the house. I looked over at Twelve. She was starting to stir. The drive back had seemed quicker than normal.

Twelve was special. We had a connection. I'd known that from the beginning. I wanted to do something special with her. She deserved it.

Twelve

I have been alone in this room for hours, days maybe. I don't know. I just know I am alone and naked. I am so cold, dehydrated, and hungry. I am too weak to move. I just lie here in a puddle of waste. I feel horrible, filthy, defiled. I no longer feel human.

I can't remember my name. Twelve? No, wait, it's Mandy, I think. He calls me Twelve because I am the twelfth woman in his collection. We're just a collection. There were eleven women before me. He loves to talk about them.

It makes me sick.

The man comes into the room. I can hear his footsteps descending the stairs. I think I'm in a basement. I am lying on concrete, and the room is always cold and damp. I can't hear anything outside. Occasionally, I might hear a thump upstairs.

The smell of stale cigarettes, cologne, and gin fills the air. I feel breathing on my face.

"By the way, my name is Lord. That's what everyone calls me anyway," he says, trying to be kind. His voice is cold as ice.

I ignore him. I am not about to call him Lord. No way! He is not my lord. I will not indulge him in his games. I don't want to play. I would much rather die than give him the satisfaction of playing. Eleven women before me played his game and died. If I don't play, I might live. Even if I don't live, I will not give him that satisfaction.

I pretend not to hear him.

"My name is Lord," he says a little louder. Again, I ignore him.

He sighs. "You will call me Lord," he says even louder.

"And you will call me Mandy," I blurt out, matching the tone of his voice. He smacks me across the face. I can feel him staring at me. I think I've rattled him some. For a moment, he seems to have lost his stride.

"You don't have a name. You're just an object. Just like these." He shoves something into my hand. It feels like a skull. I drop it.

He chuckles as he walks up the steps.

I don't know how long he was away. I thought he had forgotten about me. I thought I was going to die from dehydration and hunger. I remember thinking that out of all the things he could do, this wasn't too bad.

He comes back into the room.

"You will call me Lord. They all do in the end."

I don't say anything. I can't. My tongue is so dry it is sticking to the roof of my mouth.

"Here, eat." He puts a piece of bread in one hand and a glass of water in the other. I don't want to take it. I put the bread and glass down on the floor next to me. I just don't like giving him that control.

"Here, this will make it easier to eat." He unties my hands.

He puts the glass of water and bread back into my hands. Again, I don't take the bread, and I refuse the water. He already has complete control over me.

I remember asking the man once if I could use the bathroom. He just laughed. He actually got a nice chuckle out of it and said, "And why do you want to use the bathroom? Toilets, showers, clothing are reserved for people, for satisfying one's needs, and not for objects. Women are objects, not people. Therefore, they should be treated as such."

That was it. It felt like the end of existence. I was reduced to nothing. I was no longer a person.

I don't take the bread or the water because I don't want to give him that extra power. I am famished and parched. I don't care. I just don't want to lose that little power that I have left.

I don't feel like a person. I refuse to believe I'm an object. Instead, I am a scared animal. It kills me hearing him describe women as mere objects. I felt close to being dead. If I take the bread, it's like taking that final blow.

He has everything, and I am nothing. It's a sickening feeling.

He shoves the water and bread back into my hands. He tells me to eat. I put the bread and water back down on the floor. I want to be able to exercise a little control over my life.

The man sighs. "Fine, don't eat it. Suit yourself."

I can hear him walking away. I hear the creaking of the stairs behind him. I hear the door shut.

My hands and feet aren't tied, but I don't even bother to think that I am free, or that I even have a chance of escaping. I know I am not.

I am too weak and too tired to move. I barely have any strength left. All I have to do is remove the tape from my eyes. Then, I can see where I am at. Maybe I can even start formulating an escape plan. It requires too much energy, energy that I just don't have.

After arguing with myself for what seems like hours, I break down. I eat the bread and drink the water. I feel disgusted with myself. I am weak. I gave up everything with that first bite. With that bite, I felt like I was objectifying myself for his twisted pleasure.

I just don't want to die.

I don't want to die.

I want to live.

I want to see my family again. I miss them so much. Even Meghan. I never thought I would find myself missing my twin sister. Our personalities always clashed. We are different as night and day. It's hard to believe that we are even related. I want to see her. I want to see my family. More importantly, I want them to see me alive. I am not going to achieve that by refusing to eat and drink.

After what felt like hours, maybe even days, the man comes back into the room. He kneels down beside me. He then props me up into a sitting position. I recoil every time he touches me. I can tell that he is examining me.

"That's what I like. It's a good start," he whispers into my ear. He pulls me to my feet and pushes me up against the wall. I am too weak to do anything. He forces his tongue into my mouth as he gropes me. I don't protest. I just don't care anymore. I am too exhausted, and nothing else matters.

He has something in his hand. I can't see it, not with the tape over my eyes. Somehow, I am able to feel its presence.

"Scream for me," he whispers in my ear. His hot breath stings like acid as it hits my skin.

I don't scream. I can't even muster up enough energy to make a noise.

He sighs. "Scream for me."

I don't.

"Call me Lord, then."

I don't. I won't.

He sighs again. "Don't worry. That will change. It will all change. It always does." He forces the object inside me.

The entire time he is raping me with the object, I am thinking about my older brother, Victor, his wife, Liz, and their kids. I am completely helpless. I don't know what else to do, so I keep thinking about my family. They are an important part of me, my family. I can't imagine not having them in my life.

After a while, I stop thinking about my situation. I stop feeling sorry for myself. I've had enough of it. It has gotten me nowhere. It is depressing and maddening. It is making me crazy. I don't know what else to do. I just don't want to give him that satisfaction of feeling sorry for myself. I do the only thing I know how to do.

I think of my family. Thinking of my niece and nephew is the only thing that I can do. I love those kids. My niece, Maria, is such a little princess, never wanting to get her clothes dirty. She hates it whenever she gets her hands or her face dirty. She never likes playing in the rain or stomping in puddles. She doesn't even like finger painting. She never has. It would mess up her hands too much. She is eight now and a little diva.

Then there is my nephew, Victor Junior, or Little VJ, as we call him. He is a terror. He has me wrapped around his little pinky. He knows it too. It's been like that since the day he was born.

They are a huge part of my life. My whole family is. I long to see them again, I just want to be there for those kids and watch them grow up. They deserve that much.

They're just little kids. They don't deserve any of this. I can't imagine the turmoil my family is going through. I wonder how it is affecting the kids. They probably know something is terribly wrong but do not understand what. I doubt VJ understands what's going on. He is probably wondering why I am not there. I've been with him at least once a week every week since the day he was born.

Suddenly, I'm not there. I doubt he understands it. He's only three.

Maria would understand better. She's eight. I wonder if they are trying to shield her from all this or if they are talking to her about it.

My mind wanders back to our last family reunion. It was Maria's eighth birthday. Everyone in our family was there. It was a beautiful day. We had a nice cookout in the park. We even rented one of those moon bounces for the kids.

At first, Maria did not like the idea of the moon bounce. She was afraid of breaking a nail. Somehow, we were able to convince her. Actually, her parents, Victor and Liz, were able to bribe her. She fell in love with the moon bounce. She had a blast. It was good to see her acting like a child. It surprised all of us.

There were all types of snacks, a birthday cake, Kool-Aid and lemonade on the picnic table. Maria was thirsty. She was making her way toward the table when she tripped over her feet and landed face-first in the cake.

I can feel a smile forming across my face. To my surprise, I am laughing. I didn't think I could. I didn't think I had it in me, but I do. I am laughing.

The man stops raping me with the object.

"You find this funny?"

I don't say anything. I am savoring the memory of my family in the park. I don't want to lose it. It is the only thing that I have left.

"Well, you won't find it funny much longer," he says in a hoarse whisper. He hits me across the face with the metal object. He then leaves. I can hear him stomping up the steps.

My knees buckle underneath me. I fall to the floor. I roll over to my side. I start coughing and spitting out blood. My jaw feels like it's about to shatter. I can barely open my mouth. It's too painful.

Yet somehow, I feel victorious. The man thought he had absolute control over me. He thought he could strip me of everything, even my humanity, but he will never be able to touch my memories.

For some reason, I no longer feel dead. There's a part of me he will never be able to touch, and somehow, that thought keeps me going, at least for a little while. I'm starting to feel somewhat alive again.

Almost human.

Almost.

I just have to remember that my name is Mandy.

It's Mandy and not Twelve.

The days come and go. Some days, the man will come into the basement to give me some food and water. He will leave immediately after. Other days, he will come into the basement and watch me. He will just sit there, staring. I can always feel him staring at me. His gaze bores through to my soul. I swear there are times that I can hear his thoughts.

That scares me. More so than anything else he has done to me.

I hate it when he sits there. Sometimes, he sits there in silence, contemplating. I wish he would just do whatever it is that he is planning on doing to me.

I'm not going to live. I know that. I understand that. He has made it abundantly clear to me. I just wish that death will come quickly. I am looking forward to the day I die and can no longer feel this pain.

Other days, and these days are the worst, he will come down into the basement and talk about the other women he kidnapped and killed. There were eleven women before me. None of them survived.

"You know, I like you. I like the games that you play. Everybody has a breaking point. Everybody breaks. It's just a matter of finding their breaking point. I have never had an object last this long. Not to worry, I have something very special planned for you. Very special. You will love it. I'm sure. You deserve only the best." He laughs. There is no warmth left in his voice. I can't help but wonder when that disappeared.

I try not to listen to him. I try to tune him out. He makes it difficult. The more he talks, the more horrible I feel. These days, I have trouble remembering my friends and family. He makes sure that the only thing I remember is him and nothing else. These days, life has become much colder and bleaker. These days, I have a hard time remembering my name. All I know is that I am Twelve.

I just want to be a little kid again and wake up from this horrid nightmare. As a child, whenever I woke up from a bad dream, I would always climb into my parents' bed. My dad would always make the monsters go away. My mom would always protect me. They always made the monsters disappear. They would make me feel safe again.

I do my best to dwell on that memory and the feeling of safety and warmth. I try and dwell on the memories of my family and friends as well. I want any memory that has some type of warmth and happiness to it. I want something that will make me laugh.

Laughter is somehow salvation.

When the man talks, it is always about his previous victims. Sometimes, I get sucked into his web. I just sit and listen to him. I dread those days where, no matter what, I can't tune him out.

Those days, I concentrate on one word.

Twelve.

No. No. Mandy. My name is Mandy.

Monster

Twelve was laughing. How could she? How could she find all this funny? Nobody else would have laughed. All I wanted was to make her scream. I wanted to break her. Instead, she just laughed in my face.

She just laughed in my face. God, she is so irritating. Why couldn't she be like the rest? That's okay. It's okay. From the start, I knew she would be different. I knew she would be a challenge. It was something that I was looking forward to. I was looking for somebody different. I never thought I would make her laugh, though. I made her laugh! She must be sick if she is enjoying all of this.

As punishment, I leave her in the basement for two days. On the third day, I visit her. I give her some food and water. She takes it grudgingly. I can tell that eating the food is an internal struggle for her. I love watching her eat. It gives me a boost of confidence.

I write everything down in the notebook that I keep. I record everything about her and all of our conversations. I keep notebooks on all of my objects. I catalogue their fears and emotions. I am very meticulous in what I write. It's how I like to remember them. I love going back and reading these books, especially when I am having a bad day or an off day. They always cheer me up. It's a nice stress relief.

I come and visit Twelve in the basement. Not every day, but when I am bored or have some free time. I don't always bring her food or water. She needs reprogramming.

Some days, I will just sit in the chair on the other side of the room, watching her. I don't talk to her. I just sit there and watch. That always makes her feel uncomfortable, more so than anything else I do to her. I swear there are moments I can hear her thoughts. We definitely have a connection. There is no doubt about that. I knew there was a spark the first time I laid eyes on her. I just didn't realize she would be so aggravating. That's true of all relationships, though.

Other days, I come in and talk in great detail about the other eleven objects. I want Twelve to know the others. I want her to understand her importance. I want Twelve to feel what the others felt. It is important for me to make her understand why she is significant to me. She needs to understand why the other eleven objects are important to me. They're my life. I love them all. I love Twelve the most. I love the game. It's a great way to relieve stress.

I sit in my chair in the basement and read aloud from the journals, describing them in as much detail as humanly possible. On such days, I can see Twelve deflate.

Maybe if she understood the horror that I can inflict, she wouldn't laugh anymore. She doesn't understand what I am capable of doing. If she did, she wouldn't talk back to me the way she does.

She needs to learn respect.

It irks me that she doesn't show me the proper respect.

"How can you just torture and kill those women?" Twelve asks me one day, her voice filled with disgust.

Like always, I inhale, hold my breath for ten seconds, and then exhale. We go through this all the time, it seems like. I then patiently explain to her: women are not people. They're more like robots programmed to believe that they are people and have rights. They need reprogramming.

The difficulty of the reprogramming depends on the stubbornness of the woman.

You have a woman. First, you have to strip her of her name. She becomes an it, maybe even a number, but the number is only a means of keeping the objects apart. Next, you strip her of her clothes. You keep her locked up. She does not have the right to use the toilet or to bathe.

She no longer has the right to food or water. Why should she? Why waste food on these objects when millions of people all over the world are starving to death each year?

That's exactly how I explain it to Twelve.

"Why are women objects and not men? It doesn't make sense. We both are living, breathing creatures. We both bleed. We both need food and water to stay alive. What's the difference?" She asks. I would hold my breath and count to ten. I then start over, trying to explain it to her.

"It's not the same. Plants need oxygen to breathe, and they grow. It doesn't mean it's a person. Women are the same way. Look at the way women dress and the way they show off their bodies. Look at the media- they tell us that women should be vied for. If a woman disrespects a man, she will be punished. These women know it. They accept it and enjoy it. No actual person would want to be treated that way."

"That's pitiful. What happened to make you this way?"

"Nothing happened to me. You make me sound like some type of deviant. I am not."

I walk up the stairs and out of the basement. She irks me. She keeps finding flaws in my logic, though. I never imagined that an object could be so dense! It's maddening. At the same time, I do enjoy it. She keeps me creative. Where the others bored me to pieces after a short while, she keeps me on my toes. Twelve's been my addiction.

I tell Twelve that she should be more like Gabriella, object number two. I read Twelve the journal I kept of Gabriella. I keep diligent records—I'm methodical in everything that I do—observing everything and writing everything down no matter how small or minute the detail is.

Gabriella.

I first met her at the park.

Gabriella.

I actually like that name. It is bigger than she was. She was an overweight, short young woman.

I was leisurely walking around the park, enjoying the beautiful day. I saw Gabriella retying her Nikes.

Somebody called her name. I presume it was a friend of hers. I moved over to the nearby bench and watched them chitchatting. After a few minutes, her friend walked away.

Gabriella started jogging.

She didn't want to. You could tell that she was forcing herself to. Her eyes were saying that all she wanted was to go home and plop down in front of the TV. Instead, she was out jogging.

Everybody has a story. I wondered what her story was.

Fifteen minutes later, she was back in my view. I noticed that whenever somebody would say hi to her, she would look down at the pavement. She wouldn't say hi back. She wouldn't even smile. She would not acknowledge the person in any fashion.

She seemed to be painfully shy. I was under the impression that she wished that she was invisible.

I found that enticing, and I knew at that moment that she would be mine. Number Two. I could make her invisible to the rest of the world. The only person who would see her would be me. That suited me just fine. I know that would suit her. It was what she wanted.

I was still sitting on the bench as she passed by. She tripped over her own feet and fell. I stood up and walked toward her.

"Are you okay?" I asked, offering her my hand. She glanced up at me. She didn't say anything to me, and she ignored my offer to help her up. Instead, she went back to her jog. She had a slight limp. I guess she'd twisted her ankle.

I followed her. I wanted her to join my collection. Every now and again, she would glance back at me. She would tense up every time she saw me.

We were at a large park. It had three big parking lots. I knew we were meant for each other when I followed her into the same parking lot that I was parked in.

I couldn't believe my good fortune. Her car was parked right next to mine.

She opened up her car door. She was so tense when I stood next to her. She was shaking. I smiled at her.

"Nice day, eh?"

She ignored me. She held her breath, looking like a deer in headlights. I wanted to say something else to her, but I didn't know what. Instead, I just smiled and got in my car.

I could see the relief in her eyes when I started to drive away. She was starting to relax some. I chuckled with excitement. She was mine.

Two. From then on, that would be her name. Two. Her regular name would no longer exist. Names should be used for people. Not objects.

Two.

She would know me as Lord. After all, I am all mighty and powerful.

I was still in the park when I pulled over to the side of the road. I wanted to follow Two. A few minutes later, I saw her car. I made sure there was some distance between us before I started to follow her.

I watched her for days. At first, it was exciting, but she lived a quiet life. She didn't seem to have any friends. She seemed to be generally afraid of everybody around her. She didn't trust anyone. I don't think she even trusted herself.

A week later, I followed her into the parking lot of a 7-Eleven. I waited for her to enter the store. I parked in the spot next to hers and followed her in.

She seemed to be having a bad day, one of those days where, if something can go wrong, it will go wrong. She kept fumbling with everything she touched. She ended up dropping her purse, and its contents went flying everywhere.

"Here, let me help you with that." I gave her a reassuring smile. I knelt down and started to pick up all her credit cards, cash, and makeup. "Bad day, eh?"

She gave me a half-smile and mumbled a few words that I couldn't hear.

That was the first time I saw her smile. We walked out of the store together. I walked her to her car. I remember making some bad joke about how we were parked next to each other.

Somehow, for whatever reason, that seemed to warm her up. We must have spent a good ten minutes standing out there in the parking lot, just talking and joking. The lot emptied. There were no security cameras.

"It was nice meeting you." Her voice was quiet and warm. She turned toward her car. As she did, I pushed her into the side of it, catching her by surprise. I grabbed the back of her hair as hard as I could, and I bashed her head into the car. I kept slamming her head over and over, as hard as I could, until she finally stopped fighting. Her body seemed to have had enough.

I put her gingerly in the back seat of my car. I tied her hands and feet together with fishing wire. I drove back to the house.

I carefully carried her to the basement. I untied her hands and feet. I undressed her, exploring her entire body with my hands and mouth. I couldn't wait for her to scream for me. I retied her hands and feet together.

I called a taxi to take me a block away from the 7-Eleven. I walked the rest of the way. I needed to dispose of her car before it drew attention. Honestly, I don't remember what I did with her car. I was just too excited about getting back to the house. I couldn't wait to hear Two scream.

Twelve

There are times I have no problem tuning him out. In a sense, I am free to think about anything. The monster might have complete control of my body, but he will never have control over my mind.

I always think about my family and the last reunion we had.

Now the man is talking, and I can't bear to listen to him anymore. He is describing what he did to one of his objects. He is horrible. Horrible. I'm convinced that he is not a person but the spawn of the devil. He just drones on and on about the monstrosities that he committed against the eleven other women. All of it was justifiable to him. He doesn't see anything wrong with it.

I just stop listening. Many times before, I couldn't. Sometimes, it was just impossible to stop listening. Today, though, I have no problem tuning him out. My mind wanders back to Maria's eighth birthday party, which just happened to be the family reunion.

Maria was always a prim and proper little girl, serious all the time. She was making her way to the picnic table when she tripped and landed on her birthday cake. Everybody around her started to laugh. She stood up, pouting. She was so upset that she started to throw pieces of cake at everybody. Somehow, a full-blown food fight broke out.

Maria wasn't too happy about it, but by the end of the day, she was laughing. Everybody was covered head to toe in food and Kool-Aid.

That was a great day. It was a ridiculously funny moment. Thinking about it always makes me smile. Somehow, I find myself laughing out loud. Again, it surprises me. It also surprises the monster. He stops talking in mid-sentence.

"You find all this funny?" he asks.

I don't say anything. I just grin. I can't help it. The whole situation seems somewhat comical to me. The man has done his best to strip me of everything, memories and all. It is all a game to him. Anything that makes me laugh scares the hell out of him.

"You are a real sick bitch. That will change."

He storms out of the room. I can hear his footsteps echoing as he leaves. I am one up on him. No matter how hard he tries, he cannot steal my memories. Though he came close several times, overall, my memories are something he's never been able to touch.

For whatever reason, that gives me a bit of hope.

Eventually, the man comes back into the basement. He bends down next to me. He starts to trace the contours of my face with his finger. I hold my breath, dreading whatever he has planned.

"You know, I knew you were going to be different. I just didn't realize how different. That's okay. I just can't believe that you find all this funny. If you find this funny, just wait for what I have in store for you. I'll give you something to laugh about." He chuckles. His voice has never sounded so sinister.

He pulls me to my feet and then pushes me onto the bed.

"You will find this hilarious. I really think you will."

He stands over me. I can hear him undoing his belt. He's laughing to himself. I start to break out into a cold sweat. I'm terrified.

He starts to whip me with his belt.

I try not to cry, but I am in so much pain that I can't help it. Tears just pour down my face. I cry out with every lash, and I squirm around in the bed, trying to protect myself.

He hits every part of my body, my head, face, back, legs. Every time the buckle hits skin, I can feel it gouging out pieces of flesh. The man laughs every time the belt buckle hits me. Tears stream down my face. I scream in agony.

"Ahh... Ple...please... AHH...stop...pl... Ahhh," I whimper out during the lashing. I beg him to stop.

He laughs the entire time. After what seems like eons, he stops whipping me.

"Now, wasn't that funny?" I can hear the smile in his voice as he gets on top of me.

I cry the entire time. I feel defiled, contaminated, as if I am some type of filthy disease. I am no longer real. I only exist in a sick, twisted fantasy. I break down; I fight back, and I beg him to stop.

I do everything that he wants me to do. More importantly, I do everything that he needs me to do. I might as well be dead. I am no longer alive. I become an object, and I satisfy his need.

I vomit.

He stops.

"Now, that was perfect, wasn't it?" he whispers in my ear. "I told you that everyone has a breaking point. You were the hardest. That's what I love. It makes the experience that much better, don't you think?" he shoves his tongue back into my mouth.

I gag.

He gets off of me.

"C'mon, I know you enjoyed it. How could you not? That was the best. You know, we can enhance the entire experience if you just call me by my name. Come on. Call me Lord."

I don't say anything. He smacks me across the face.

"Call me Lord."

"No!" The sound surprises me as it escapes my throat. For a moment, the monster seems confused.

"You will call me by my name. I am Lord. I am almighty and powerful. You will come to realize and respect that." He disappears for a couple of minutes. I can hear the jingling of his belt when he comes back.

"Call me Lord," he says again.

"No."

He hits me with his belt. It strikes me against the head and face. Suddenly, sound disappears. I become extremely lightheaded. He whips me again and again, hitting my arms and chest.

This time, I don't beg him to stop. I refuse to. I don't even cry out.

"Call me Lord," he says again. "You will enjoy it more, I promise."

"So, is this how you killed the others, by beating them to death?" I don't know what makes me say it.

A part of me wishes that he would just end it. I am just so tired of everything. All I want is to die. I have already made peace with my God.

Honestly, I think that is what I was trying to do when I said it. I want him to kill me. At least then, I won't be living in this hell. I know he's going to kill me anyway. I just want him to hurry up and get it over with.

"What?" He sounds insulted. "What do you mean? I have never killed anyone before."

He begins to pace back and forth.

"Right… And those eleven women before me just magically died, then?"

"I'm not a murderer."

"Then how did those women die?"

"I don't hurt people. It's only a game. You're only an object."

"What about the others? Were they objects too? Well, they're not. They were living, breathing human beings."

"I have never killed anyone. Never!"

"Are you that fucked up that you don't know they were people? They were people! You killed them. You murdered them. All those PEOPLE would be alive if they'd never met you! Hell, I would still be alive if I'd never met you!"

"SHUT UP!" He stops pacing. I can feel his hot, rancid breath on my face.

"You are a real sick bastard. I guess you have to be to murder—"

He picks me up and slams me against the wall. He hits me hard across the face. My jaw feels like it has shattered. I can't open my mouth. I can't speak.

I can feel his hot breath on my face.

"I am not a murderer." The tone of his voice has changed. Somehow, it sounds more evil, more wicked. He hits me again and stalks out of the room. The stairs creak one last time.

I don't know it yet, but this is the last time he will ever enter the room. He just leaves me there, naked and filthy, with my hands tied. I have duct tape over my eyes.

This is it. He's going to let me die alone in the basement. It's my fault that he raped me. I screamed for him. In his mind, I gave him consent. That's what it feels like. He never raped unless the women screamed first. I knew this. Yet I broke down and gave him what he wanted.

At first, I think about biting off my tongue, ending my life on my own terms. Not his. As much as I want to die, I want to live even more.

I then start to fantasize that a prince in shining armor will come and rescue me. He will be my prince charming. He will fight off the monsters, slay the evil dragon, and take me to safety. We will fall in love and live happily ever after.

I don't care who rescues me. I just want somebody to find me. I don't want to die alone. At the same time, a part of me wishes that nobody will ever find me. I can't imagine what I must look like lying there naked, covered in my own waste, vomit, and blood. I've never felt so worthless. So weak.

It is humiliating and degrading. I just want it all to end. I pray to God. I want him to take my life. I can't handle it anymore.

I can't move. I have problems breathing. I can't stop shivering. My skin aches. I don't ever remember being in so much pain. After hours, days maybe, I start to drift in and out of consciousness.

Everything goes black. I can't keep a single thought in my head. I am no longer in pain. I can't feel the cement underneath me. It seems that I only exist in the darkness.

My prayers are finally answered. I die.

I'm positive about this. I hear voices. The sound is sweet. It's like music to my ears.

"…S…She…She's over here."

"…Stay…w…with…me… Everything…is going…to be…okay… You're safe now."

I can't make sense of what they are saying. The words are coming out all jumbled. My mind is numb. I can't make out the voices. I just know one thing. I died.

Monster

I had Twelve begging for me. The sound of her begs and screams was so beautiful. We really have a connection. I knew she felt it. Our coupling was extremely gratifying, not just physically, but emotionally too. I knew she felt what I felt. We were on the same page. It felt like we were on cloud nine.

That was the best experience ever. Then she had to go and ruin it! She totally ruined the mood. She accused me of being a murderer. I'm not! She told me I was fucked up because I don't know what people are.

I know what people are! Men are people. Women are objects.

I hit Twelve across the face and stormed out of the basement. I wanted to kill her. She is so irksome. It bothered me what she said. Instead, I went for a drive, clearing my head. The others knew their place. She will come to know hers too. I'll make sure of that.

I feel the need to prove to Twelve that I can be a decent person. As I am driving around, I see a payphone. I didn't know they still existed. It feels like a sign. I use the payphone to call 9-1-1.

***

I watch from a distance, hidden by the shadows. It is late at night as I watch the police entering John Smith's house.

I wonder how long it will take the cops to find her. When they do, will she still be alive? I hope so. The suspense is wonderful. It makes my heart race.

I kept John Smith's house for over a decade. I didn't want to let it go. I made such good memories there. I'm going to miss that place. I am glad that I never brought any personal items to that house, though. I kept that life separate. I'm going to miss it. I'm going to miss my trophies.

I light up a cigarette and continue watching. A small part of me hopes that Twelve will be dead. She pissed me off too much. She was too defiant. She definitely has a mind of her own. I couldn't reprogram her. I never met anybody with such resilience.

All the other women were easy to reprogram. All I had to do was strip them of their clothes, refuse to let them use the toilet or to bathe, and give them just enough food and water. They became very compliant.

It was becoming quite boring actually.

Twelve is different. I knew she was going to be from the beginning. I find her alluring and confusing. Even with the humiliation and deprivation, she would still laugh. How could she still laugh?

Is she that messed up?

Twelve is maddeningly exciting.

A part of me needs her to be alive. We have a connection, a spark that was extremely evident during sex. That spark helped set the mood before Twelve ruined it.

She has to be alive. I can't imagine life without her.

I need her to know that I called the cops. She called me a murderer and a monster. I am not, but if that is the game she wants to play, so be it. She wants to see a monster; I will show her a monster. I can become whatever she wants me to be.

In the distance, I can hear sirens. It sounds like music. It's one of the sweetest sounds. It sounds almost as sweet as objects begging for their lives.

I walk across the street and slide into the driver's seat of my car. I put the keys in the ignition and start the engine. I light up another cigarette. I take the ambulance as a good sign. The cops found her. She's still alive. I can feel it. We have a connection. I knew from the very beginning.

I phoned the police and left an anonymous tip. I did it for Twelve. She called me a murderer, and that really bothers me. I have never hurt a fellow man before, let alone killed one.

Twelve's an object, just like the rest. They were all objects, pawns, just waiting to be sacrificed. All the other women knew that. They all knew they were objects. They even accepted it the moment they called me Lord.

Twelve's the only one who couldn't accept it. It's a game. All of life is. She's a pawn. Why can't she just understand that?

That is something she would never accept. She didn't play the game properly. She refused to play by the rules. In fact, she changed the rules without me even realizing it.

I never had a problem before, liberating women so that they could see what they really are—objects to satisfy a man's wants and needs.

I do hope Twelve survives. I will make sure she understands that I left that anonymous tip. I think it will help her accept that she is an object and I do have absolute power and control over her. She is not going to win. Not at her own game. She made me lose my game. Now, I am going to make her lose hers.

Twelve

I know one thing.

Death is marvelous! I can't feel any more pain. In fact, I can't feel much of anything. I am lying on something soft and warm. It feels like I am floating on a cloud. I think I am. I'm in heaven now, and nothing can ever hurt me.

I am safe and warm. There is light all around me. I hear a voice. It is soft and kind. I can't make out the words. The voice is just filled with so much warmth. There is something reassuring about it.

Everything around me is hazy. Nothing makes sense. For the first time in a long time, I feel contentment and warmth. I never thought I would feel warm again. I am in heaven. Nothing else matters.

My prayers have finally been answered.

I hear more voices. They are jumbled up and sound as if they are coming from a distance. It doesn't make any sense.

"Is she going to be okay?"

"You're safe now."

The voices sound familiar. It's disconcerting at first. The more I listen to the voices, the more I realize they sound like those of my family. How can that be?

I am dead.

I passed that horrible test, and now I am in some small corner of heaven.

I'm in a daze. Everything is making less sense. That is my dad talking. How can that be unless he died too?

I slowly open my eyes and utter, "I'm alive?"

"Yes, kiddo. We're here. We're here."

Both of my parents are talking in between their sobs of relief. They always seem to speak in unison. I can feel my mom's hand gently going through my hair. I can smell her perfume, a hint of Chanel No. 5.

My dad's hand is resting reassuringly on my shoulder.

"It's going to be okay now. Everything is going to be okay. It's going to be okay. It's going to be okay now. Everything is going to be okay," he keeps repeating. I'm not sure who he is trying to convince.

I'm not dead.

I am not dead. I have a hard time wrapping my mind around that.

This is not heaven. It's a hospital.

I am still alive.

Everything is slowly making sense.

Slowly.

I just want it all to be over. I want to be dead. I don't want to be alive. I feel so much shame for thinking that.

As much as I love my family, as much as I prayed that my family would see me alive again, I am really disappointed when I realize I am still living in this realm of earth and not in the kingdom of paradise.

Everything hits me like a bag of bricks. I feel dirty and filthy. Everything that happened was my fault. I knew something was off that day. I dismissed it. I ignored my instincts.

"If you see any odd behavior, don't dismiss it. Go with your instincts." That is what my brother Victor and his wife, Liz, are constantly preaching. They own their own Kenpo karate school. That is their number one rule: go with your instincts.

That is great advice, and I ignored it. Not only that, but I screamed out and begged him to stop. He needed me to do that. I did. I hate myself for giving him everything that he wanted.

Oh my God, what if he gave me an STD? HIV? What if I'm pregnant? I cry. I feel so hollow inside that I might as well be dead.

"You're lucky that somebody called 911 and left an anonymous tip. Another day or two and… Well, if we hadn't found you when we did, you probably wouldn't have survived."

That is so hard to cope with. I don't feel lucky. I feel cursed. I don't want to be alive. I wish I wasn't. I wish he had killed me. I don't know how or why I survived.

I spend three weeks in the hospital. I barely remember any of it. I don't remember all my injuries. I don't remember the multiple surgeries. I remember the pain. I don't remember the broken bones, internal injuries, or lacerations all over my body, but I do remember the pain.

I remember him. I remember his face, the sound of his voice, the way he smells. He is a white male in his mid to late thirties and of average height and weight. He has brown eyes and wild brown hair. He looks like every other white male. He didn't stick out. There was nothing special about him.

His voice always sent chills down my spine. It reminded me of ice. It lacked warmth, kindness, and compassion. It was cold. He always reeked of stale cigarettes, cologne, and gin.

I remember him. I don't think I will ever forget.

I remember the cops, medical personnel, and my family bombarding me with millions of questions. I answer them to the best of my ability.

After a while, the faces of all the people at the hospital—the cops, doctors, nurses, my family—meld together.

I do remember the detectives questioning me. It's horrible. They want to know every morbid intricate detail, from the day I was kidnapped to the day I was rescued. They are gentle with their questions. They are so kind and understanding.

I tell them everything that I can remember about the man, Lord, everything that I saw, heard, and felt. Everything except for the journals and wishing that I was dead.

I wish I knew what his real name is. I seem to know everything else about him. He is one man I will never forget. He is a monster.

I tell them about the eleven women before me. I'm afraid it's not much. My brain wants to shut down. It doesn't want to work. My memory is shattered. It's like somebody has given me a thousand-piece jigsaw puzzle and ordered me to put it together without telling me what it's supposed to be. I might be able to figure out a piece here and a piece there, but overall, it doesn't make sense.

I was in that basement for six weeks.

It was only six weeks.

It feels more like a lifetime.

I thought about my family, my siblings, VJ, Maria, and my parents during that horrible time. I tried to think about them. I did my absolute best to remember them. The monster made it hard to remember. I was determined not to forget.

I couldn't remember my name. He had me questioning everything about myself. The only name I could remember was Twelve. I shut down. I forgot my name. Truthfully, I didn't want to remember it. I just wanted to be anywhere else. I wanted to be anyone else.

When I wasn't thinking about my family, I was thinking about death. Nothing else mattered. I wanted to die. I kept debating if I should kill myself. I thought a lot about seeing if I could actually bite my tongue off. I wondered how long it would take to exsanguinate.

I couldn't bring myself to do it.

I didn't want him to win.

I couldn't allow him to win.

I'm hoping the cops will be able to figure out who the bones in the basement belong to. I don't know what closure means, but the other women's families deserve to know what happened to their loved ones.

I feel like I knew these women, like they were close friends of mine. The man would describe them in such intimate detail. I can see their faces.

He spent so much time reading from his journals. I don't know if he kept the journals at the house or someplace else. I know that I should mention them to the cops—in case they don't know about them. It could help to uncover who this monster is. I am too ashamed to. It's too embarrassing, so I keep quiet. He degraded me in every way imaginable.

I have no idea why he let me live. He could have easily killed me like he did the others.

"Why did he let me go?" I keep asking anybody who will listen. No one has an answer, at least not one that is satisfactory. There were eleven other women before me who didn't make it. What made me special? I don't know. I don't know why he let me live.

I feel guilty that I am alive and the others are not. I feel bad for the family of the eleven women who died. At the same time, I feel somewhat envious of those women.

They are dead. I am not. Dead is what I want to be. I don't want to cope with my new reality.

I remember when I first came out of my fog-like state. It seemed like everyone in my family was looming over me. They all seemed so relieved to see me alive. The memory makes me feel ashamed. How could I think about death and suicide?

Six weeks.

Six horrible weeks.

Six weeks, he had me locked up in the basement, torturing me, raping me. It was only six weeks. I don't believe it. It was an eternity.

As I look at everybody in my family, they all look as if they've aged several years. They look awful. They all have bags hanging under their eyes. It looks like they haven't slept for a long time. They probably haven't.

I thought about my family a lot when I was locked up in the basement. I wanted them to see me alive. I feel bad for them. It never occurred to me what they were going through, the stress of not knowing.

I'm not prepared.

I look up at my twin sister, Meghan. She's crying. It actually surprises me. I know it shouldn't, but Meghan and I have never liked each other. We love each other because we are twins. We tolerate each other because we are sisters. If we weren't blood, we would absolutely loathe each other.

"Always the drama queen, ain't we?" Meghan says, winking at me. That makes me smile.

I can't believe how terrible she looks. She looks as if she's aged more than our parents. It makes me wonder what I look like. We probably no longer look identical. I refuse to look in the mirror. When he whipped me with the belt, the buckle kept hitting my face. I had to have reconstructive surgery. I can't bear the thought of looking at myself.

The monster jacked up so many lives, more than anyone will ever realize. The police have no idea who he is. That scares me the most. He's been kidnapping and killing women for over a decade, and nobody knows who he is. I just pray he doesn't hurt anybody else.

I wish I knew his name. I only knew him as Lord. That is how he introduced himself to me.

Lord. I refused to call him that. I refused to acknowledge him in any way other than the monster that he is.

"That's probably what kept you alive," somebody at the hospital told me. I don't remember who it was. All the faces and voices blur together.

The days at the hospital blur together too. Everything seems to be one long, gigantic nightmare that I don't think I will ever wake up from.

One night, near the end of my stay, after everybody leaves the hospital, I am lying on the hospital bed, listening to the hum of the machines. I concentrate on that sound. I still feel dead, and the sounds of the machines keep me tethered to this life. That's how I think of it.

I hear a sound. It doesn't belong with the noises of the hospital. I recognize it, though. It sends shivers down my spine.

I hold my breath.

Listening.

I try to convince myself that it can't be. Not here. Maybe I'm dreaming and don't realize it.

I hear it again.

Goosebumps break out all over my body. My hands and feet go numb and cold.

The sound is barely louder than a whisper. I hold my breath. It's the only thing I can do to keep from freaking out.

"Twelve."

I don't move. I don't say anything. I keep my eyes tightly shut, trying to figure out if I am imagining it or not. I can't tell.

"Twelve, I'm here." The smell of stale cigarettes, gin, and cologne infiltrates my nostrils.

Minutes pass. There's no talking, just the murmuring of the machines. His smell is still there, assaulting my senses.

Is he actually there? Am I dreaming?

Suddenly, something brushes up against my arm. I nearly jump out of my skin, screaming and kicking frantically.

"Mandy. Mandy, It's okay." The voice is soft and soothing. I don't understand. It's not the voice of the monster, but he's here with me. I flail chaotically, trying to get away from him.

Why doesn't anybody stop him?

Why doesn't anybody help me? They have to know that he is here. They have to know that I am in danger.

"Mandy…"

I feel myself calming down. I don't want to. I need to get away. I have to get away, but I can't get my body to work. My mind is fuzzy again.

"Mandy, everything is going to be okay…"

I can't figure out who this Mandy person is. That is not my name. It's a memory from a previous life.

Twelve is my name.

No, that's not right either.

That's not right. I don't know.

I am so confused. I don't know what's going on.

Somehow, the police are here. They're asking me questions. I don't feel lucid enough to answer, but I do my best to. Again, I describe everything from the encounter. What he sounds like, smells like. I kept my eyes shut. I was afraid to open them.

The police scour every inch of the hospital. Nobody is able to find him. It doesn't surprise me. He's been doing this for over ten years. He's good at it. He doesn't make mistakes. I have the impression that nobody believes me about the encounter. They were just indulging me.

Honestly, I don't know if he was there. I don't know if I was hallucinating or dreaming the whole encounter. I don't know. It feels so real, though.

Monster

Twelve has been in the intensive care unit for several days. It scares me. Things seemed to be touch and go there for a while. I want her to survive. I need her to.

At some point, I remember being in the waiting room. Her family was there, waiting anxiously to hear from the doctors.

I recognized her family immediately from the time I spent in Twelve's house when I was still getting to know her. She'd had pictures of every member of her family plastered all over the walls and on the tables.

I brought on the fake tears and sat down next to Twelve's father. Her mother was spending her time harassing the nurses. She wanted to know if Twelve would live.

"We will let you know as soon as we find out. For now, she is in surgery. The doctors here are the best. They will do everything in their power… I know it's hard, but right now, you have to be patient and let them do their jobs."

Her mother did not seem satisfied with the answer and continued to harass the nurses. Her kids were trying to calm her down. The youngest son kept apologizing to the staff. I was elated when Twelve's father engaged in conversation with me. I told him my son was in surgery. That he'd cracked his skull open from a skateboarding accident. He hadn't been wearing a helmet.

Twelve's father opened up to me. I listened intently and pretended to act concerned when he started talking about Twelve and about what had happened to her.

"If I ever meet the bastard that did this to my girl, I will kill him."

I entered into a euphoric-type nirvana when he started rambling about what he is going to do to the bastard who had done this to his daughter. It was so hard not to laugh. If only he knew.

I couldn't believe that I'd never realized the joy of talking to the families of my objects. It created a euphoria so much greater than having them call me Lord. It reinforced just how powerful I am.

I'm ecstatic when I learn that Twelve is going to survive. She will live, but I want to make sure that she doesn't survive. She wants me to be that monster that she described, and I will be. It's going to take some creativity, but I will be. I don't want to disappoint her. I will be whatever she wants me to be. I just need her.

She spends three weeks in the hospital. As do I.

I wander the halls, engaging in small talk with everybody that I see. I want to learn everything that I can about Twelve and her recovery.

I overhear the doctors telling her and her parents that if she'd been undiscovered for another day or two, she would have died. That pleases me to hear that. I'm not done with her yet.

She is never left alone for any length of time. She is constantly surrounded by family, cops, nurses, and doctors. It's really frustrating. I just want to spend some alone time with her, and I can't.

Even though I can't get any time alone with Twelve, I see her parents around the hospital. We only talked the first night, when I officially met them. All of the other times we've met, we've just exchanged pleasantries, just the regular hellos and how are yous.

Before I acquired Twelve, I went to an online spy shop. I used John Smith's credit card to buy some listening devices and had them shipped to John's house. I wasn't sure if I would ever need them. Twelve was different from the rest, and I wanted to be prepared.

I'm glad that I had those bugs in my car when I made that anonymous tip to the police. I pride myself on always being prepared.

I couldn't get to her when she was in ICU, but I'd figured I wouldn't be able to. When she was out of recovery, she had her own private room. When her parents stepped out for just a second and Twelve was in a medicated state of unconsciousness, I snuck in and planted the bug in her room.

I want to know everything about Twelve. I need to know everything about her. I can't think about anything else. She is perfect. I want to set the mood again when she's ready. Not only did I find her physically satisfying, but emotionally too. I'd never felt that way before.

I need to know what she is telling the police.

The detectives come in and question her. They too want to know her story and every dark, gloomy detail of her kidnapping.

I listen to her story.

I find it interesting.

I can't believe all the lies she concocts about me. She makes me sound like some type of deviant monster. The worst part is that the cops, her family, everybody eats it up. They believe her story, every part of it.

She makes me sound like the devil. I'm not, but if she really wants to play that kind of game, I will. I can become that monster she wants me to be. I can become that kind of monster that everybody thinks I am because of Twelve's lies.

All the time the detectives are questioning Twelve, she never mentions the notebooks. I'm surprised about that.

Unfortunately, the police should already know about them. I kept them in John Smith's basement. When they found Twelve, they surely found the books as well. I wonder what else they found. That entire house is now a crime scene. I'm sure, by now, they've been through it with a fine-tooth comb. I don't think I left anything incriminating at that house.

I wish I had the notebooks. Those are my trophies. Each object has its own journal. They contain the date and time of when I first saw the objects and everything that I did before acquiring them. I recorded every single thing that I did to these objects. Everything. They enjoyed every moment of it. I know they did.

I feel so stupid. I don't normally make mistakes. I'm always prepared, but I wasn't prepared for Twelve calling me a killer. She had me so frazzled. She really rattled me when she called me a murderer. She thinks I'm evil. I whacked her in the face and left her in the basement with my notebooks. Those notebooks help keep me calm.

I wanted to go back, but I couldn't face Twelve. I basically phoned the police on a whim. I wanted to show her compassion before showing her what evilness really is. I should have made sure that I had those notebooks in my possession before making the call. I wasn't thinking straight.

I wish I had my notebooks. I just want to compare what she is saying to what's in the books. She's making me sound diabolical. Her version of events is horrible. I have a hard time listening to it. It makes my stomach queasy.

I'm half-tempted to turn myself to the police just so I can set the record straight. It's hard not to say anything to the cops, especially as I'm standing by the elevators waiting when I see the detective walk out of Twelve's room. He, too, stands near the elevator with a newspaper in his hand, waiting.

I nod.

There's a ding, and the elevator opens. He goes in first, and I follow. I push the button for the ground floor.

"What floor?" I ask.

"Same."

"It's rumored that this girl"—I point to the front page of the paper—"is in this hospital. Do you know anything about that?"

The cop doesn't say anything. He just gives a quick, involuntary jerk of his head.

"God, that poor girl. I feel so bad for her and her family. What type of bastard would do that to somebody? Seriously, hearing about these heinous acts makes me sick."

The cop takes the bait. He says, "I hope I'm the first to catch this motherfucker so I can put a few rounds through his head. You asked who would do such a thing to another person. Only monsters do. It's pure evil."

I have to bite my tongue at that. I am close to telling him who I am.

For the record, I am not a monster. I do not hurt people. I have never hurt a man in my life, let alone killed one. I don't think I would be able to. It's immoral.

As a teenager, I would kill small animals, cats and dogs mostly. I was conducting scientific research, collecting data on my findings. I always had an interest in anatomy and the sciences. Anyway, what's the difference between dissecting a cat on your own or in a biology class in school?

Cats are not people. Women are not people. Women are objects. They should not have any rights. Why can't people understand that?

Growing up, nobody cared about what happened to my mother. She was brushed aside like a piece of trash. She would always go back to John Smith and the others. They would beat her senseless and would do horrible things to her.

I tried getting her away from that life. She never listened to me.

"You're too young to understand. When you're older, you will," she would always say. I do understand. Women are objects. They're only objects. They enjoy being treated as such.

I really don't understand all this concern for Twelve. She's only an object.

I just want the police to know the truth: I'm not a monster. That's going to have to wait, though. The game isn't over. I lost my game, but Twelve wants to play a new game, and that's what we are going to do. She's telling everybody I am a monster. If that's the game she wants to play, then so be it. A monster is what I will become. After all, I don't want to disappoint her.

Twelve

The next day, I wake up with a doctor talking to my parents. When they notice I am awake, everybody stops talking. Talk about awkwardness.

"Hi, Mandy. I am Dr. Logan. May I sit?"

I nod. I've never met Dr. Logan. Her voice is filled with warmth and kindness. It's funny, and that's the first thing I notice about people now. Not so much the sound of their voice, but if it's filled with warmth or coldness. Everything about her is inviting.

"I heard about what happened last night. I want to talk to you about it. Is that okay?" I hesitate but then nod my head. I don't really remember last night. My memory is so shoddy lately.

"Do you want your family to stay while we talk?"

I look over at my parents. I'm confused by the question. I'm confused by the compassion.

"It's up to you, Mandy. Whatever makes you comfortable. You've been through unimagni—"

"I want them to leave," I blurt out, interrupting the doctor. I hate talking about what happened in front of my family, especially my parents. My mom always breaks out crying. It's hard for them to deal with. I try to spare them from that horror. My parents leave the room.

Dr. Logan stands up and closes the door behind them before sitting back down next to me.

"What happened last night?"

I tell her everything that I can remember. It's so frustrating. I can't tell if it is real or a bad dream. I do have nightmares every time I sleep. I dream about him, his touch, his smell. In these dreams, I keep giving him what he wants—I freak out, scream, fight back. I tell Dr. Logan this.

"Do you think last night really happened?"

"I don't know. How would he know where I am? How can he be here and not have anybody know it? It just felt so real, though. It's crazy. I don't know what's going on. I feel like I'm losing my mind."

"The nurse's station is right outside of this room. Only a minute or two passed from the time the nurses heard you screaming last night to the time a nurse was in the room to see what was going on. The nurse didn't see anybody leave or enter the room. The cops searched the entire hospital. They didn't see anything out of the norm. Now, I'm not saying it didn't happen. It might have. I don't know, but another possibility: sometimes things like this happen after traumatic events. It is called a traumatic dream. Some people have nightmares that are exact replays of the trauma that was experienced. It feels so real because the dream is replicating the trauma. When we are asleep, our body is paralyzed. It keeps us safe from acting out our dreams. However, for people who have experienced trauma, this protective mechanism breaks down. It causes us to enact aspects of the dream while we sleep..."

I stop listening, pondering what she said. Doctors keep telling me how important sleep is. That it will aid my recovery better than anything else.

Maybe it was a dream?

I don't sleep. I can't. I have nothing but nightmares. I dream about him and the basement. The other women. I didn't sleep for the six weeks I was locked in the basement. I cat nap in the hospital. Every time I start to drift off, I see his face. Monsters that lurk in the darkness plague my sleep. I hate these nightmares. I keep waking up with a profound sense of fear. I feel very anxious, and my heart races. I'm all sweaty and cold.

Dr. Logan tells me that I will be discharged in the next day or two. She gives me a list of therapists in my area as well as support groups. She also gives me a list of online support groups.

She prescribes me prazosin . It's not a sedative. It blocks some of the effects of adrenaline released in my body, which may help reduce nightmares and sleep problems. I am told that the effects can take a day to a couple of weeks to start working.

It takes effect right away. The rest of my stay at the hospital is peaceful. The monster doesn't show up again.

I am also thrilled to learn that the STD tests came back negative. I don't feel toxic, just filthy.

Monster

I can't resist. I need to see her. I miss her so much. It's been a long time. To touch her again would be bliss. I no longer have my notebooks, so I can't look over Twelve's journal. I never realized how much I relied on those books. I feel like I am going through withdrawal not having them.

Twelve is so intoxicating. She makes me feel great. It was paradise listening to her scream… Now, all she has to do is call out my name during sex.

She will not call me by my proper name, Lord. I wish she would. That will enhance the entire experience for both of us.

Nobody is around. I sneak into her room. I have to see her. I'm drawn to her. Twelve is sleeping, or maybe trying too.

"Twelve," I whisper out to her as I stand there watching over her. She doesn't respond in any way. I wonder if she heard me. I don't risk saying her name louder. I don't want anybody else to hear me. They will only try to keep us apart.

I move closer to her.

"Twelve," I whisper. She tenses.

"Twelve," I say again. She is so beautiful. I want her. I need her.

"Twelve."

She doesn't open up her eyes. I know she hears me. She tenses up even more. She stops breathing, holding her breath. I'm torn. I want to touch her again. I know she wants me to.

Even though she is aggravating, she is even more exotic and alluring than anybody I've ever met. I can't help myself.

"Twelve. I'm here."

I touch her arm.

She freaks out, screaming and flailing frantically. It's exciting. She's screaming, just like before. I go to kiss her, but out in the corridor, I hear feet pounding down the hall in our direction. I hear voices. I can't hear what they are saying because of Twelve screaming. They're coming to check on her. I know it.

I don't have time to leave the room, so I hide in the bathroom, barely making it there in time. I don't want anybody to see me. The game has just begun. I am not ready to give up Twelve. I'm going to have so much fun with her. She will enjoy it.

Doctors and nurses are in the room. They try to calm Twelve down. She is fighting them tooth and nail. Kicking, flailing, and screaming. It is arousing to watch, but I don't stay. With all the commotion, I am able to sneak out of her room.

I leave the hospital.

I'm disappointed that I can't spend more time with her. It's okay. I have her room bugged. I can just listen to what is going on. It's not the same, but it's something.

I feel so giddy. I've never felt this way before with anybody else. She just brings out the best in me. I think about her constantly. I think about the way she looks. She has the most beautiful body. I think about the way she feels. Her skin is soft and smooth. Maybe not anymore, but she has the most wonderful touch. I think of the sound of her voice. I replay all of our conversations.

I will destroy her.

***

It's exciting to see her mentally deteriorate. She really has no idea if what happened last night was real or a dream. She's leaning on the dreaming side, especially after talking to the doctor.

She has been prescribed medication for her nightmares. I figure this could work to my advantage somehow. I'm not sure how yet. I'm not done with her. I need to become that monster that she wants me to be. After all, I can't and won't disappoint her.

I can't wait for her to be discharged from the hospital. I just want to have some alone time with her. I need it.

I'm looking forward to quality time with Twelve. I want her to suffer. She is an object. I couldn't break her in the basement. Some days, I would come close, but I could never really break her.

No matter what I did to her, she would just laugh. I can't wait to wage psychological warfare on her. That's what Twelve wants, for me to be a monster. In order for me to be that monster, I need to destroy her mind. It's the only way that I can think of that will work.

I hope that it will break her.

I'm enjoying this game. It's a completely new experience for me. It's exciting. It hasn't gotten boring yet. I don't think it will. I'm having fun with it.

She likes it too. I know she does. I can feel it. I knew we had a connection the first time I laid my eyes on her. I can't wait for her to call me Lord, and she will call me Lord. I am the evolution of mankind. I'm perfect in everything I do. I will become perfect at this game too. She will know it.

Twelve

"If you don't have any more questions, I'll be back. Let me go get the discharge papers." The nurse walks out of the room.

I'm being discharged! I am actually able to leave this hospital and go home! I can't wait to get back to my house, my neighborhood, my job, my life. I want to put all this behind me. I want to forget it all and go back to my old life.

My parents and Jason are here with me, waiting. They're talking to me, but I'm not listening.

I'm thinking about how great it will feel to take a nice, hot shower. I can feel him in me and on me. I want to scrub it all off. Afterward, I am looking forward to a nice, hot bubble bath. It's been too long. Six weeks was spent lying in my own waste. How mortifying. Three weeks spent in the hospital washing with a basin of water and soap.

I feel filthy.

I can't wait to get home and to shower to finally get clean and the bath to relax.

"When we get back home we can…"

What is my mom talking about? I'm not going back to my parent's house. She is making it sound like I am.

"Wait. What? I'm going back to my house."

"Oh, Mandy, you've been through hell. It's okay to come back home for a while. Let us take care of you until—"

"No. No. No. I'm going back to my house. I always loved that house. I just want to go back home."

"Mandy, you've been through multiple surgeries in the past couple of weeks. The doctors told you to take it easy for a while. C'mon, it's not like you would be permanently moving in with us, just until you're recovered enough."

"No. I can't. Right now, it seems like my entire world is unraveling. I just have to get back to normality. Going back to my house is the only way to do that. Anyway, if I go with you guys, it's like the monster is winning."

"Mandy, that's not…" My mom's voice trailed off. She's starting to get upset but is trying to hide it. She keeps looking over at my dad for help. He is quietly standing in the corner, pretending to be fascinated with something on his shoe.

That's when Jason speaks up.

"She won't be alone at her house. I'll be with her. You guys have been driving me bonkers anyway."

I start laughing. That would be normal. Jason is nineteen and living at home. Jason and our parents don't always see eye to eye. When that happened before, he would always disappear to my place or Victor's. Victor always charged him rent. I don't.

It would be just like old times but without the horror films.

***

I'm home, but it's not that great. The first thing I did was take a shower. I scrubbed and scrubbed and scrubbed, but I still feel filthy, contaminated, and toxic. That shower wasn't great. I felt too exposed standing there naked like that. I skipped out on the bath.

I just want to jump back into my old life, but I can't. I can't. I just want to get back to work, but I follow the doctor's orders.

Everybody at my work has been really great and supportive. I can get my old job back whenever I want it. I can go back whenever I feel like it. I can work either from home or the office.

I was always a gamer. That's what I loved. It was always my dream to be a video game designer. I was good at it too. Thinking back, I can't remember if I actually enjoyed my work or if I was just going through the motions.

I want to go back to work.

I have no desire to go back to work. I don't know what I want. I feel like a walking contradiction.

My friends, family, neighbors, and coworkers keep visiting me. It's great, but I hate it. It makes me feel alone. I feel so isolated when I am around people.

I took it easy for two months, but I was bored. I decided I needed to get back to living. I was physically feeling better.

I went back to work. I tried, anyway. I couldn't. I was too terrified to leave my house. I couldn't bring myself to. Just in case. I don't ever want to relive that experience. I don't think I will ever get over it. How can you deal with something that horrible?

I tried working from home. I couldn't. I had lost all motivation. It was like the more I tried to get back to my old life, the more my brain wanted to shut down. I don't want to do this anymore. I can't imagine ever wanting to go back to designing video games.

Or playing video games.

I hate my neighborhood.

I hate my house. I no longer feel safe here. I want to. I refuse to give it up.

It's a shame. The house is a cute little thing. I was so proud of myself when I bought it. I was so excited. It was my home. It felt like it too. It was safe. The whole area was safe.

Now, it feels tainted and dirty.

Instead of being a place of solace, it's a place of hell. Lately, everywhere I go is hell. It's a constant reminder. I won't let him win. I love this house. I want to make it work.

I'm scared. Always. I don't sleep. It's not because of nightmares, but because I feel disgusted with myself. I want to be dead. I don't deserve to live. I wish I had the guts to end it myself.

I make an appointment with my primary care physician. She suggests that I stay on prazosin. She also prescribes Ambien to help me sleep and an antidepressant.

I take the antidepressant, but I hate the way it makes me feel. I'm all jittery and can't stop shaking. I also have racing thoughts. After a week, I stop taking it. The shakiness goes away. I hate drugs. I do try the Ambien. I just want to sleep. I need to sleep. I don't remember the last time I slept.

I just need sleep.

Ambien is great! It numbs my mind to where I can't feel anything. I'd rather not feel anything than feel everything. It does put me to sleep. It knocks me out for well over ten hours. Nothing really wakes me. I might stir for a few minutes. Then I'm out like a light again. That's the beauty of Ambien.

I don't know if I'm dreaming or not. I don't remember. My brain went up and quit. Since then, my memory has been shoddy and fuzzy. The nightmares are back. I think. I don't know.

***

He wants me to scream. He needs me to.

"Come on, let me hear you scream," he says. I can feel his hand on my throat. I can feel his lips exploring my body.

"Scream for me," he says.

I don't. My mouth feels like cotton. It's so dry. I can't speak.

"Scream for me using my name," he says, thrusting against me. His one hand is around my throat. He uses his other hand to continue exploring my body.

I lie there, frozen in fear, my eyes tightly shut. He squeezes my throat. I am gasping for air. My lungs are on fire. He's going to kill me.

He's finally going to kill me. I start sobbing, praying that I will wake up from this horrid dream.

"Scream for me," he whispers into my ear. The stench of stale cigarettes, gin, and cologne is nauseating.

"Scream for me—just like old times." He forces his tongue into my mouth and continues thrusting up against me.

I force myself to scream as loud as I can. I hope that the sound of my voice will finally wake me from this nightmare.

"That's a good girl," he says, caressing my face.

He takes his time.

***

The brightness of the sun shining into my room wakes me up. I'm lying in a fetal position, trembling like a leaf. My heart feels like it is going to explode; it's pounding so hard. My hands and feet are so cold that they are numb, and it feels like I have an elephant stomping on my chest. I stare at my pajamas lying in a heap on the floor. I don't remember taking off my clothes. I'm frozen.

I can't move.

It's happening.

I wonder if the prazosin has stopped working. Maybe the nightmare was just a fluke. This is the first nightmare I've had since I started taking prazosin.

The doctor did say that people who have experienced trauma have a tendency to enact aspects of the dream while they sleep. Maybe that's what I was doing. I was not permitted to wear clothes in the basement. Only people could wear clothes, not objects.

I was an object. That thought still makes me sick.

94

Monster

Twelve is finally out of the hospital! My heart skips with joy. I don't think I've ever felt so happy. I am going to have so much fun with her. I need to become that monster she keeps describing me to be. I can't wait to be able to spend some quality time with her. It's been a long time since we've been alone together.

Right before she was discharged, I put listening devices in her house. I'm not really expecting her to go home. I thought, after what she had endured, she would move back home with her parents. It's wonderful to discover that she's back at her house.

Her brother is staying with her. That's okay. I know that house like it's the back of my hand. I spent so much time there during our get-to-know-each-other phase.

It's a nice split-level house. She has a bedroom downstairs that her brother uses. Her bedroom is upstairs. It will be tricky sneaking in and getting to her. Leaving will be easier. When I was still in the getting-to-know-her stage, Twelve would sometimes crawl out her window and sit on the roof, which slightly slopes. She would stare at the sky. Now, she keeps all the windows and doors locked. I like that. I bet her neighbors do the same now.

I like the fact that she can still surprise me. The others, after a while, bored me to tears. Not Twelve. She keeps me on my toes.

I'm glad she decided to go back to her house. That's romantic. Going back to where we first met.

I want her. I need her. I can't get to her, though. For being a workaholic, Twelve sure seems to know everyone under the sun.

It's frustrating. She doesn't make any time for me.

For the first several weeks, people constantly surrounded her. As time goes on, people visit her less and less, which I like. I can't wait to start spending some alone time with her.

It is great listening to her talk. She's trying to get back to living, but she's having a difficult time adjusting. She can't work. She wants to. She tried to. She just couldn't do it. She doesn't go outside anymore. When she has to leave her house, she always has somebody accompanying her.

It does surprise me that she wants to go back to her house. That is where I acquired her. It is her house, though. She worked hard for it, earned it. It's a sign that, yes, the economy may suck, but if you work hard and do not give up, you can live the American dream. It's her way of rubbing my face in the dirt with her cockiness.

It is her way of telling me that she will not break. That she will not address me by my proper name, Lord.

I follow her one day to her doctor's, then to the pharmacy, and then home. Her doctor prescribed her some sleeping pills. They knock her out. Apparently, she sometimes sleepwalks but can barely remember anything.

I wonder if I can get her to scream for me again in her drug-induced state of mind. I wonder if she will remember.

I find it very stimulating to sneak into her house. My heart is pounding in my ears. I love that feeling. It reminds me of being on a rollercoaster. I hope her brother is a sound sleeper. I creep into her room. She is so beautiful.

I touch her face. She doesn't even stir.

I remove her covers. I find it vexing that she is wearing clothes. I carefully remove them. I explore every centimeter of her body. I forgot what she looks like, smells like, feels like. I whisper her name.

She opens her eyes and then closes them tightly. I am still exploring her body. I want her to scream for me. I need her to scream for me. I talk to her. Unexpectedly, she starts screaming, giving me consent. I pray it won't wake her brother up.

It feels so romantic, so fulfilling. It meets all my needs. She beat me at my game, but I'm winning at hers.

I wonder if she will remember any of this. A part of me hopes she will. I want her to know that no matter where she is, I will always have complete control over her body.

She is mine. One hundred percent. I'm not going to let her go. I can't.

Twelve

He wants me to scream. He needs me to. I do. I did. It was my fault that he raped me. I could have prevented it. I just had to stay quiet, but instead, I begged him to stop. I just couldn't handle the pain anymore. I wanted him to stop whipping me with his belt. I allowed myself to be raped. I don't think I will ever be able to forgive myself.

I can feel him in me. I can feel his lips exploring my body. Even now, months later, I can feel him. His smell of stale cigarettes, cologne, and gin is trapped in my nose. That's all I can smell. I swear that's what my room smells like.

No matter how many showers I take and how hard I scrub, I will never be clean. I feel so disgustingly dirty. I'm filth.

I can feel him crawling on top of me. It's the same damn nightmare. Over and over again. "Hi, Twelve. Miss me? I missed you. Scream for me, Twelve," he says.

I don't.

"Scream for me," he says, thrusting up against me. His one hand is exploring my body. His other hand is around my throat.

I lie there, frozen in fear. My eyes are tightly shut. He squeezes my throat. I am gasping for air. My lungs are on fire. He's going to kill me.

He's going to kill me.

He's finally going to kill me. I start sobbing, praying that I will wake up from this horrid dream.

"Scream for me," he whispers into my ear.

"Come on, Twelve, scream for me—just like the other day." He forces his tongue into my mouth and thrusts up against me.

I force myself to scream as loud as I can. I hope that the sound of my voice will finally wake me up from this nightmare.

It doesn't.

He takes his time, having his fun with me. He's violating me all over again.

I've had enough. I can't handle this anymore. I feel like I'm going to die if I don't wake up.

Somehow, I work up enough courage. I finally do something different this time. I fight back, screaming for help, hoping Jason will hear and will be able to wake me up from this hell. I'm kicking and screaming, flailing like my life depends on it.

***

"Mandy! Mandy! Are you okay? Mandy!" I hear footsteps.

I don't respond. Who is this Mandy person? I'm confused and disoriented. I have no idea where I am. Am I trapped in a basement, maybe? I don't think that's right. I am lying on something soft, not hard. That sickening smell of stale cigarettes, cologne, and gin assaults my senses.

Therefore, I have to be tied up, naked, in that basement. He was calling me Twelve.

I'm Twelve.

No, I'm not Twelve. Or am I?

No. Twelve is not a name.

I'm Mandy. The voice confuses me. It takes me a second to realize it's Jason. So, I am home. I am not in the basement. I open my eyes. I'm lying on my bed, but my blankets and pillow are on the floor.

"Holy shit, Mandy! What the hell?" Jason says as he covers me up with my blanket.

It takes me another minute to realize what he means. My clothes are in a heap on the floor. I'm naked, shaking like a leaf. Not from the cold, but from terror.

Jason runs to the window. He's talking. I don't know what he's saying. His head is out the window. Did he open the window? I don't remember seeing him open it. Did I open it? I don't recall. I normally keep everything locked. He's on the phone. I don't know who with.

He throws his cell phone down on my bed and sits down next to me.

"Mandy, what happened? Talk to me, please."

"I had another nightmare about him. About the assault."

"Shit! Mandy, I don't think it was a nightmare. It smells like cigarettes in here. I heard you screaming, and as I approached your room, I heard a man's voice. It was muffled, and I couldn't hear what he was saying. When I came in here, the window was wide open. I called the cops. They're on the way."

I'm retching all over. It wasn't a dream? It had to have been. There is no way I would allow him to abuse me all over again. I find myself sobbing. I don't think I have ever felt so toxic in my life. All these nightmares I've been having weren't nightmares after all?

I feel nauseous. Oh, God. Again, I empty the contents of my stomach all over the side of my bed.

"It's okay. We're going to figure this out," Jason says. He has his arm around my shoulder.

Suddenly, I realize I'm naked under the blankets. I feel so exposed. Especially with Jason sitting there. I want desperately to take a shower. I'm covered in this monster's filth. How does my baby brother not find this repulsive? I find it repulsive! I can't understand why people want to be around me. I don't want to be around me. I find myself tensing up, frightened. Jason stands up.

"Hey, Mandy, he's gone. It's just us. The window is closed and locked. I'll wait outside your door so you can get dressed. The cops should be here soon. Okay. I will just be on the other side of the door if you need anything. It's going to be okay."

Monster

I make it to safety, barely. That was a close one. It's exhilarating. I feel like a teenager again. Sneaking around a girl's house, hoping her parents won't catch me. Instead, this time, it's her brother.

I really love the medicine Twelve is on. It is easy to sneak into her room and strip the clothes off her. She barely stirs. It takes a lot to wake her, but when she does, that look of utmost fear and confusion is worth it.

I'm not even sure if she remembers these encounters when she wakes up the next day. If she does, she's never spoken of them.

I was really getting cocky. I wasn't expecting Twelve to fight back. I really didn't think she would be able to under the influence of the medication. She punched me square in the nose. She kicked me in the groin, but missed. I started cursing her out. I was still straddling her. I was about to hit her back when I heard her brother racing up the steps, calling out her name.

I jumped off her and ran toward the window, unlocking it. The window stuck for a second when I was trying to open it. Luckily, I was able to jar it open, and I crawled out onto the roof. The roof slants downward. I cautiously walked down it and jumped off. It wasn't that far from the ground.

I hid behind the bushes in Twelve's yard. I could see her brother popping his head out the window. He couldn't see me, though. It was too dark.

It's been a turbulent relationship, but overall, I'm glad Twelve is mine. I wasn't planning on taking her. She wasn't exactly my type, but she was at the same time. I am so pleased I have her. She rejuvenates me. I can't wait for her to become totally mine. I wish I had my collection. At least I have Twelve.

I went over to her house for three nights. Every night, she would do what I wanted. It was always great. What made it so pleasurable was that Twelve had no idea if this was actually happening or if she was dreaming.

I put listening devices in her house. I never did hear her mention these encounters to anybody. She never left her house. It was our own dirty little secret.

I find that romantic.

I love being able to toy with her.

I do love that medication. It makes Twelve unsure of reality. I was able to get what I wanted, both for me and for her. I need Twelve to feel like she is losing her mind. I need her to question everything about herself, including her sanity. When I am through with her, the only thing she will not question is me. Lord.

She will call me by my proper name.

Lord.

All of the other objects did.

The cops were called.

It is my fault. I became too complacent. I got too loud, and I allowed Twelve to do the same. Next time, I have to make sure not to get too cocky.

I'm glad I decided to bug her house. I feel more connected with her.

The cops arrive. I listen intently. They are questioning Twelve, but it sounds more like an inquisition. They have my journal of her with them.

They did find my journals, after all. I knew they would, but I was hoping that they wouldn't.

They read bits and pieces of the journal to her and ask her questions related to the passages.

Did she know she was being stalked for six months? I don't like that word. It has a negative connotation to it. I wasn't stalking her. I was getting to know her better. That's not stalking. There's a difference.

Did she know that I actually tried talking to her?

Did she know that I spent a lot of time in her house?

They keep bombarding her with question after question. Twelve does nothing but cry and whimper. It's a beautiful sound.

I'm disappointed that my notebooks were found, but I am glad at the same time. These journals prove that I am not diabolical or evil. That it's just a game. At least it will set the record straight. However, listening to the cops, they still make me sound evil. I'm not! I have never hurt a man before!

That's Twelve for you. She has everybody convinced that she is a victim in all this and that I am the devil's spawn. I will become that monster that she wants me to be. It's a game, after all.

Twelve has to take responsibility, though. She is enjoying the game. Why else would she scream for me? Why else would she go back to the place we first met? Why else would she not tell anybody about our couplings? The answer is simple. She is enjoying the game as much as I am. She likes the chase. The chase is thrilling, exhilarating. I enjoy it too.

I do miss those notebooks. I never really realized how much I relied on them. I've been thinking of starting another journal, for this new game that I am playing with Twelve. It's not the same. I'm afraid to. What if I lose possession of those books? I don't think I could handle the stress of not having those journals.

I stop listening to the questions. I keep thinking about my objects. Without the journals, I'm starting to have a difficult time remembering how I acquired them. I do hope that these journals don't have any personal information in them. I don't think they do. I'm pretty sure they are all about the objects.

Notebook three might be a different story. There might be personal information in that one. I don't recall. Three almost ruined me. I was stupid with her. It was an impulse thing. Normally, I study the objects, their habits, and behaviors, anything I can possibly think of before taking them.

Three was definitely spur of the moment. I was there. She was there. It just happened. She was wearing a nice, slinky dress with shoulder straps and high heels. She was on the side of the highway. Her car had a flat tire. She was on her cell phone, trying to call somebody.

Something was wrong. Maybe her cell phone battery was dead, or there was no reception. She was dressed so nicely. It looked like she had an important function that she was trying to get to.

I figured I would be a good Samaritan.

I pulled up behind her. I got out of the car and asked her if she needed help or wanted to use my cell phone to make a call. She seemed relieved at first. She didn't know how to change a flat.

This is where I wish I had my journals. I said something, or she said something. I don't know what happened. I don't remember. Suddenly, she became very prickly towards me.

I don't know why, but at that moment, I wanted her. I needed her. She was very, very attractive. I felt drawn to her like a moth to a flame. The more I talked to her, the more uneasy she became. The more I found her irresistible.

I needed her to become mine. I wanted her to become part of my collection. Without thinking, I attacked her. Right there on the side of the road. I don't know what I was thinking. I just wanted her. I wanted to know, I needed to know, what she felt like.

I knew, on some level, she wanted me to. She barely fought back. I was able to force her into my car. It was actually somewhat disappointing. A few people saw this transpiring. They pulled over to the side of the road. One person was on his phone.

The other person came running towards me. I don't remember what he was yelling. I wasn't paying attention. I was too busy getting Three into the passenger side of my car. I ran around to the driver's side, hopped in, and drove off before the man could get to me.

That was the sloppiest that I have ever been at acquiring my objects. I vowed to myself never to be impulsive like that again. I had Three tied up and gagged in the basement of John Smith's house. Afterward, I drove my car to the ghetto part of town. I left the keys in the ignition. I also made sure the windows were down. I hiked back to my apartment.

Waiting.

I knew the police would show. I was sure somebody had been able to get my license plate number. I stayed at my abode, waiting and thankful that I kept everything about these objects at John Smith's place and not mine.

The cops did show up later on in the afternoon. I remember them asking me about my car. I told them that somebody had stolen it earlier that day. That I hadn't gotten around to reporting it yet. I don't remember much of the conversation afterward.

They took me in for questioning. They had me stand in a lineup. Neither witness could pick me out. Both said that I hadn't been there.

They let me go with apologies.

I waited a couple of days before making the trek to John's house. I gave Three water and food. I apologize for being away for so long.

I felt bad for keeping her waiting. We hadn't even had our fun yet. I kept her in the basement for a week. I didn't touch her at all. The moment had to be right. I had a mattress for her to sleep on. I made sure she had plenty of food and water.

"How are you feeling?" I asked her one day.

"Why are you doing this? What do you want?"

"You." I gently touched her face. She didn't flinch, but she tensed up. I took a switchblade out of my pocket. She gave three whimpers as she tried to hide in the wall.

"It's okay. I'm not going to hurt you," I told her reassuringly. I used the knife to cut the shoulder straps on her dress. It made it easier to get her out of her dress.

"You know you want this," I whispered to her. I was so close to her that I could feel her heat radiating from her body. I couldn't wait to touch her. My heart was pulsating so fast. I was sure she could hear it.

The unexpected happened.

She agreed.

"You're right. I want you. I want this to happen. I've been thinking about it since you offered to help me back on the highway."

She then gave me a deep, passionate kiss. It caught me by surprise.

"I want you, baby. Untie me. I can make you feel so good. I can help you fulfill any fantasy that you want." She kissed me again.

It felt like she'd cast a spell on me. I found myself untying her hands and feet. I guided her over to the mattress. She couldn't keep her hands off me.

"Call me Lord," I whispered to her, trying to set the mood.

"Lord, I want you," she whispered back.

At that moment, I lost all interest in her. I no longer found her attractive. I had not been expecting this. This had never happened to me before. Three, and the whole situation baffled me. I didn't say anything. I stood up and started to walk away.

I was in my own little world. I'd made it near the steps when she bashed me over the head with her heel. It caught me off guard. I stopped walking, feeling dazed. I had to hold on to the railing for a second, and then she charged at me. She actually tackled me, taking me to the ground. She quickly stomped on my stomach, knocking the breath out of me. She grabbed my head and slammed it on the step.

I could hear her running up the steps, yelling at the top of her lungs. She took me by complete surprise and almost got away. I was able to regain my bearings before she had a chance to leave the house.

I found her screams for help to be extremely sexy. At that moment, I wanted her. I needed her. She'd made it to the door before I caught up to her. She had it open. She was almost able to escape the house, but I was quicker and stronger. I was able to slam the door shut. I had Three sandwiched between me and the closed door.

She spun around and did her best to fight back. This time, I was prepared. I loved the way she squirmed, trying to get free. We had a good time up against the wall.

Everything happened so quickly. It was hard to enjoy it. She had to ruin the experience by doing everything I asked her to. That's how I knew that she was glad to be with me.

I became bored.

Afterward, I took her back into the basement. I tied her back up and forgot about her. I was no longer interested. I was already on the prowl for somebody new and exciting.

Twelve

The bastard was at my house. He knows where I live. I knew that. I knew that. He captured me right outside my home. He was following me that day, toying with me. Honestly, I was able to convince myself that it was a spur-of-the-moment-type thing for him.

Some of his kidnappings happened spontaneously. Those of the other women were premeditated. I always assumed that my kidnapping just happened. It's easier for me to think that way.

I went back home, to my house, because I wanted to get back to my normal life. My home was always a place of safety. I wish I knew then what I know now. I never really thought about it. It was easier to forget.

The cops question me. I feel like the world's biggest idiot. How could I not know what was happening? Why did I think it was a dream? I let him rape me all over again, over and over, just because I thought the whole thing was a dream. I hate myself. God, why am I alive? Why couldn't I have died in that damn basement?

I throw up. I am so disgusted with myself. I feel like I deserve to be raped for being so stupid. I am such a freaking idiot.

The police bring along the journal that the monster kept of me. They want to know why I came back to my house. The monster never read my journal to me. He read everybody else's. There was so much that I didn't know. There is so much that I blocked out.

It's embarrassingly painful listening to bits and pieces of what happened to me. This monster spent months and months stalking me. I never knew it. He would follow me to work, home, wherever I would go.

When I was at work, he would sneak into my house. He would take pictures of the house before rummaging through everything I owned. He would sit in my chair. Shower in my shower. Clean himself off with my towel. Sleep in my bed. Then, he would return everything back to the way it was.

I was oblivious.

I had no freaking idea.

The police seemed so nice, kind, understanding, and respectful when I was in the hospital. Now, they are making me feel like the situation is my fault. They're right. It is my fault. I should never have come back home.

I should never have taken the Ambien. I really liked the way it made me feel—nothing. It would numb my mind. It would put me to sleep. I didn't dream. I would enter this void. Very little could wake me. When something did wake me, it was always dreamlike. I could barely remember it.

I remember him. I remember everything he did to me and said to me. I didn't think it was real, though. I really didn't. I just thought it was what the doctor said was a traumatic dream.

The cops have a forensic team at my house. They are doing whatever it is they need to do. They're doing their job. I wish the cops would do the same and find this bastard.

The following weeks are foggy. I black out constantly. I have a very difficult time recalling things. I can't remember yesterday at all. Or this morning, for that matter.

They don't find any traces of his DNA or fingerprints. I didn't think they would. He's been doing this for too long. He is too good. I once saw a documentary about adermatoglyphia. It's a condition where a person does not have fingerprints. I often wonder if this is true for the monster.

He never leaves any traces behind. He's been doing this for so long and has never been caught.

It freaks me out; the police have no idea who this man is. Even after finding his journals and the remains of eleven women and one man, they have no idea who he is. I'm the only one who lived. I don't know why he let me live. I think about it every day. I hate myself for it. I feel so useless. I haven't been much help to the cops.

They told me once that I was very helpful. Apparently not enough. He still roams free. I pray each night. I pray that he doesn't snatch another woman. I will feel responsible if he does.

I don't think he is on the hunt. He's not done with me yet. He's made that crystal clear by raping me in my own home and in my own bed. God, how could I not know what was happening? I was so convinced that it was nightmares.

I stop taking Ambien and Prazosin. I'm afraid to take any medication. I don't want to take any chances. I don't want to enter that fog-like numbness ever again.

***

I'm at my house with Jason and Meghan. We are packing up some of my stuff. I'm moving back in with my parents. I don't know what else to do. It makes me feel so defeated, so broken. I just want to free myself of this monster. I don't think it will ever happen.

I feel like I'm being intimidated out of my house. I just can't stay here anymore. I bought the house less than a year before I was kidnapped. After I was rescued, I went back. I lasted three months here.

This house used to be a place of solace. Now, it's turned out to be a gateway to hell. That is how I will always remember this place.

My siblings and I are upstairs. I don't want to take anything back to my parents' house. It all feels contaminated. We are packing some clothing and other necessities when I hear a noise downstairs.

It nearly makes me jump out of my skin. Any unexpected noise scares the hell out of me. Even expected noises make me jump. Jason and Meghan didn't hear anything. I make them go downstairs with me to investigate. That's when I see the open cabinet.

I freak out.

"He's here. He's here. He's here." I keep whimpering, unable to say anything else. I start shaking uncontrollably. I must look like a scared deer trapped in headlights.

That's how I feel.

Meghan rolls her eyes.

"Mandy, you just left the cabinet open. It happens."

"He's here. He's here. He's here," I keep repeating.

I know he was here. I'm certain of it. I feel him.

"I know you have a lot going on. There is so much happening. Right now, you are fine," Meghan says, sounding exasperated.

I don't believe her. He's here. I know it. I am not going to let anybody convince me otherwise. I let the people at the hospital convince me that he wasn't there when he was. I was able to convince myself that he wasn't at my house when he was. He was in my bed with me, and I didn't know it. I'm crying nonstop. I don't know what else to do.

I stand there, frozen, staring at the open cabinet, repeating, "He's here, he's here."

Jason believes me. Maybe because he was here the entire time, the monster would sneak in and rape me. Both of us were clueless. I know he feels responsible. He stayed with me to protect me. It's not his fault. I don't blame him. I blame me.

Jason feels the monster's presence. As soon as he saw the cabinet, he was on his phone, talking to the police. He wasn't taking any chances.

Again, the cops come. Again, they go through the house. Something different happens, though. One of the officers finds a listening device. There are bugs planted in almost every room.

I totally freak out. I don't know what else to do. It feels like I have weights tied to my body, and I've been thrown into the dark, cold ocean. I'm drowning.

Meghan packs my bags while I talk to the police. My siblings and I leave the house the same time the police do. Jason drives us back to our parents' house.

I spend the next several weeks with Victor. I hang out at his Kenpo school while he is teaching. Victor is also a firearms instructor. He is really into all of that. He always has been. He tries to convince me to take karate lessons. I won't. I don't know why, either. I just don't want to do anything.

Hanging out with him doesn't make me feel safe. However, I don't feel like I am in danger.

The rest of the family spends that time at my house, packing, cleaning, and fixing the place up before putting it on the market.

I don't go back there. I'm too afraid to. I'm too afraid to be alone. When I go to bed at night, I always make sure Meghan or my mom is in the same room as me. I feel ridiculous, like I am some kid afraid of the bogeyman.

Except, it's not the bogeyman I'm afraid of, but a real monster. I don't feel safe. No matter where I'm at or who I am with, I don't feel safe. My anxiety levels are so high I can't function.

I don't know what to do. Most days, I feel like I live in a catatonic state. I don't remember anything. I don't feel anything except numbness and hatred. I hate myself with a passion.

Monster

I'm so happy that Twelve is losing at her own game. She thought she had defeated me, but she never will.

I spent all my free time at her house.

I really love seeing Twelve like this. Beaten down. Broken almost. I don't want her broken. I want her to be one hundred percent shattered.

After our last encounter, she moved back in with her parents. That's the first step to destroying her. Twelve swore to her family that she would never move back. That she couldn't because it would feel like moving backward and not forward. She wanted nothing more than to get on with her life.

Honestly, I didn't think she would ever move back in with her parents. She was just so adamant about it. She said to move in with her parents was like letting me win.

I like that.

I'm going to miss her. I'm going to miss our coitus meetings. It was always fun and satisfying in so many different ways. Twelve is exotic. It never gets boring with her. The others bored me to pieces. I doubt I will ever be able to find anybody else like Twelve.

Twelve keeps things spicy. I hope she is enjoying the new game as much as I am. This is the game she wants to play. She should be enjoying it.

The cops found the bugs that I hid in her house.

I hope nothing traces back to me. It shouldn't. I used John Smith's credit card to buy them. I had them shipped to his house, not mine.

I gave the cops John Smith's house. They already know about that. I never kept anything personal in that house except the notebooks.

I'm safe.

I already know that.

I'm better than the police. I have been doing this for so long. The police are still clueless. They always will be.

Other than our coitus encounters, I would sneak into her house and do things like move the glass of water that was on an end table in the living room to the kitchen table. Or open up a cabinet.

By doing little sneaky things like that, I made Twelve really start to question her sanity.

She had no idea what was real and what wasn't. Neither did her brother, for that matter. I love gaslighting her.

I'm going to miss our encounters, but I am glad she moved back in with her parents. She no longer swaggers when she walks. Instead, her head is down, and her eyes dart to anything that moves. Her shoulders are hunched.

She has stopped walking. She never goes out anymore. And when she does, it is normally because someone in her family has forced her to go to her therapy appointments.

I'm there for her every step of the way. I am always around, watching my prey. I already established my presence when Twelve still lived in her house. I've eased up some now that she's moved in with her parents.

I don't want her family to know that I'm here watching. It's hard getting into the house with all the people around, so I watch from a distance. I don't want anybody to see me, not even Twelve. I like toying with my objects. I want to give her a false sense of security.

She consumes my every thought. For whatever reason, I obsess over her. More than normal, that is.

I watch her from the shadows when she is at her parents' house. I follow her to her counseling sessions, keeping to the parking lot.

One day, I am in the parking lot at her psychiatrist's office, sitting in my car, puffing on a cigarette. The window is cracked a bit. I'm thinking about Twelve and how counseling seems to be helping her. I'm in my own little world, thinking of creative ways to change all that, when I hear Twelve's voice, and it brings me out of my reverie.

"I am not going back," she says almost inaudibly, but the sound of her voice travels in the near-vacant parking lot.

I put out my cigarette and roll the window down a little farther so I can hear better. I sink down as far as I can in the car. I don't want anybody accidentally seeing me. I can still see them, though.

She is with her brother, Victor, and her sister-in-law, Liz. They stop walking.

"Why not?" Victor asks.

"She's a quack. She has no idea what she is talking about."

"Who? Your counselor? She's the best in the area when it comes to something like this."

"That's bullshit. She doesn't have any experience with any of this. How the hell can she know what I am going through when she has never experienced any of this herself? I am sick and tired of her patronizing me!"

"You seem to be doing so much better these last couple of months. I really think she's helping you."

"She's a freaking bitch who thinks I'm paranoid or something. She wants to shove goddamn pills down my throat. She says that will help. Bullshit! The last time I took pills, he kept… He kept, and I didn't know… How the hell did I not know what was going on? Yes, I've been kidnapped, held captive for weeks, beaten, tortured, and raped. Then raped again in my own home, in my own bed. She makes it sound like the whole thing is my fault. I already know it is…but she doesn't need to keep…"

I hold my breath, hanging on to every word. It's unusual to hear Twelve freak out like this. It's wondrous when she does, though.

"Why does she think you are being paranoid?" her brother and sister-in-law ask in unison.

Twelve takes a deep breath and tenses up some. She quickly scans the parking lot. She doesn't see anybody, and she fumbles and stumbles over her words a bit before answering.

"Be…be…because I…I see him." Her voice is almost inaudible. I really have to strain to hear her.

"See him?" Again, Victor and Liz speak in unison, with alarm in their voices.

"Yeah, well…well, not exactly. Like, right now, I know he is here. I can feel him staring at me. I can feel the intensity of his gaze. It makes me feel… Well, he's here, yet I don't see him."

"Do you think he is following you around or something?"

"Yeah, it's possible."

"Unlikely."

"No, he's here."

Twelve's brother grabs her by the shoulders. His voice is stern when he speaks. "Mandy, listen to me. That bastard has either moved on to his next victim, is rotting in prison, or, better yet, is lying dead someplace."

"Listen to me, sweetie." Liz touches Twelve's shoulder, and she flinches. I've noticed that she flinches every time somebody touches her. I love seeing it. I love seeing her trying to pick up her shattered life.

"You heard what the detective said. They have his notebooks. They know how he thinks, how he feels. He always moves on with all his victims."

"Yes. AFTER he kills them! I'm still alive. The game is still on! He always said he had something special for me. What if this is it? He kept sneaking into my damn house and…and…he's probably doing the same at our parents. I'm never going to be safe for as long as he's out there."

"Yeah, you're right. You are the only person who has survived. He didn't kill you. Why? Because he is dead or is in prison."

"Or he has something else planned for me. God, nobody is freaking listening to me! He has something special planned for me. He kept telling me that from the start. Anyway, who else would have left that anonymous tip? It was him. I know that as fact. Just like I know for a fact that the sun always rises in the east."

"It's been six months. It's okay to think that he's here. After all, he put you through unimaginable hell. Anyway, I haven't seen anyone or anything suspicious. Liz, have you?"

"No, I haven't."

"See, Mandy. I also know for a fact that Mom and Dad haven't seen anything suspicious either. If you had seen him around, we would have too. The only time you are alone is when you lock yourself in your room, and your windows are always locked, with the blackout curtains always shut. Anyway, there is always somebody at the house."

"Maybe, but Victor, every fiber in my being is telling me that he's here, watching, calculating, waiting for his next move. Anyway, what about the hospital? He was there. What about at my house? He was there. He wouldn't just disappear now because it may be inconvenient for him."

"True, but he hasn't done anything to you in six months. Even if he is around, you have to get on with your life. You can't let him control it."

"Maybe, but I am never going to talk to that bitch, I mean quack, again."

Twelve turns away from her brother. She mumbles something else, but I can't hear it. I have never seen her so frustrated. Listening to the conversation has made my day. She won my game, but she is losing at her game.

I'm elated that she can't stop thinking about me. I knew from the first time I saw her that we would have a special bond.

***

I decide to leave Twelve alone. It's been almost a year. It's hard. I want her more than anything. I'm still watching her from a distance with binoculars. I don't go anywhere near her or her family. I'm staying safe, biding my time, waiting for that perfect moment.

I don't want to lose that special bond that we have. I don't want there to be any awkward moments when we are together again.

I want her to feel a sense of peace. Well, maybe not peace, but I want her to think that I have forgotten about her. I want her family to feel it too. I want everybody to forget what happened, or at least bury it deep. I'm looking forward to the day Twelve and her family start to live normally again.

I don't know why, but I just want everybody to think that I have forgotten about Twelve. I will never forget her. I think about her night and day. I even dream about her. I'm not done with her. Not even remotely close. She loves me. She screamed for me.

She loves the game.

She will scream for me again. She will call me by my rightful name, Lord. The game doesn't end until she does.

It's boring, though, not being with her.

I decide to take a risk. I buy Twelve's house. Actually, I convince a James Chantaz to buy her house. Or at least to put his name on the mortgage and all the paperwork. He's some stranger I met at a bar. He was down on his luck. I made him an offer he couldn't refuse: ten thousand dollars cash.

Twelve, and I had so many good memories there. I can feel her presence in the house.

I no longer have my journals. This is the only way that I know of to remain close to Twelve.

Twelve

I was always a strong, confident, social person. I was a go-getter. If I said I was going to do something, I did it. I had everything I ever wanted in life. Then, in a split second, it all changed.

I'm broken now. I wish I were dead. That's all I think about. Death.

I can't bring myself to go out. He's there. I know it. I'm too afraid. I just lie in bed, staring up at the ceiling. I can no longer keep track of the days.

According to my parents, it's been a year since I have seen any sign of the monster. Yet I can't relax. He's out there. Waiting. I'm still trapped, waiting for him to finish his game. I know he's around. There are times I catch a whiff of him. Stale cigarettes, cologne, and gin.

My family is normally pretty supportive, but right now, I get the impression that everybody is walking on eggshells around me. There is a rift between us that was never there before. It could be just me, though. I don't know.

I've been sulking around my parents' house, afraid to live. I am so pissed off at them too. I remember how, as a little kid, they would tell me that monsters don't exist. They were so very wrong. Because of that, I blame them for what happened to me. It's easier that way.

It's been twelve months since I was rescued. I find that ironic. Twelve and twelve. The man who calls himself Lord is still out there. I am still convinced that he is following me around. Everybody thinks it's very unlikely.

Except for Jason. He's on my side. It feels like he is the only one.

I don't know. I just know that my thoughts, actions, and perceptions have totally changed. I'm not sure for better or worse. My entire personality has changed.

I have lost the ability to connect with other people. I feel so disconnected from life and from reality. I find it difficult to trust other people. Those I used to trust, I no longer do. I push everybody out of my life. At least, I try to.

I haven't been able to find a good therapist. I stopped trying after the last one, six months ago. The last therapist seemed like a good fit at first. But then she started insisting that what happened was my fault. She's right. I saw odd behavior. I dismissed it. I ignored my instincts.

If I hadn't, I would still be living life. My entire world has unraveled. It is the darkest, loneliest feeling in the universe. I feel so alone and so lost.

I went to the support groups a couple of times. I don't like going. It's a constant reminder. I don't like listening to the other's stories. More importantly, I don't like telling mine. I keep thinking that if I ignore the whole thing, it means it never happened. If I talk about it, it becomes real. Too real at times.

I can't handle it.

I break down. Disassociate.

I can't stand being alone. I can't stand being around people. Every single noise makes me jump out of my skin. Yet I'm afraid of the silence. I swear, at times, I can hear him calling out my name. Twelve. I try to forget. That's not my name anymore.

It's exhausting.

I never felt so tired in my life.

When I look in the mirror, I no longer recognize the person staring back. I don't remember the last time I took a shower, washed my hair, or changed my clothes. I don't remember the last time I brushed my teeth or the last time I ate.

I want to make myself repulsive to protect myself. I don't ever want this to happen again. That's a lie. The monster had no problems kissing me and having sex with me when I was in the basement, covered in my own waste, vomit, and blood.

I make myself repulsive because that's how I feel. I'm a disgusting, revolting, vile, pathetic excuse of a human being. I don't deserve to live. There is this constant, overwhelming sense of doom smothering me. I can't break free from it.

I wish I had the guts to end my life. If I do, he will win. I will not let that happen. I can't let that happen. That is the only reason I don't attempt suicide.

I move through the house like a ghost. I don't do anything. I don't clean. I don't go out. I don't take care of myself. I don't sleep.

I'm in my room, lying on the bed, staring at the ceiling. That has become my normal, everyday activity. I find it exhausting. The windows are closed and locked. I have blackout curtains. They are covering the windows. I can't tell if it is day or night, and I don't care.

I hear a soft rap on my door. It makes me jump, but I don't answer. I just lie there, wishing for whoever is behind the door to go away. I am not in the mood to socialize with people. I don't think I can even be nice to somebody. I just want to lash out. I want everybody to hurt as much as I do.

The only contact that I have with people is with my family. Even that contact is extremely limited since I lock myself in a room and stay there day and night.

The knocking is a little louder.

I don't say anything.

I just want to be left alone!

Normally, a closed door is a sign that the person in that room wants to be left alone. Victor, his wife, Liz, my parents, even Meghan don't seem to understand that. They're always knocking on the door. They're always letting themselves in. They are regularly letting me know that they are there for me always.

I can't handle the badgering. It's too much stress. They want me to go back to therapy. They want me to attend the support groups. I know that they are just worried. I must be in bad shape when even Meghan is worried. They're trying to give me a gentle nudge in the right direction. It feels like a shove off a cliff.

It's overwhelming. I shut down. I can't function. I don't know how to. I'm afraid to try therapy again. I can't put myself out there like that again. Drugs, hell no. They are out of the question.

The only activity that I am capable of doing is to stare up at the ceiling. I don't sleep. I go days without eating. I don't care about my hygiene. It's not that I don't care. These everyday, mundane activities are way too stressful for me to handle.

It makes me shut down. It's exhausting.

The knocking gets louder and more persistent. I forgot somebody was knocking. The door creaks open a crack. I'm ready to lash out when I hear Jason's voice.

"Err, Mandy, can I enter?"

I don't respond.

I find myself relaxing some. Jason is the only one who doesn't get on my case. He doesn't treat me any differently. He basically ignores me. Which is fantastic. He is the only person who seems to respect my boundaries.

"Mandy, I'm coming in. Okay?" He doesn't give me any time to respond. He opens the door all the way and walks in.

"C'mon, you gotta get dressed," he says in a very chirpy voice as he opens the curtains. The room floods with brightness as he lets in the afternoon sun.

My response is to hiss at him.

Jason sits on my bed.

"Come on. You have to get up, take a shower, and get dressed. We are going out. And I am not taking no for an answer." Something magically appears in his hands. He gives it to me. That's when I realize he is actually bouncing on the bed with excitement.

"I got you backstage passes to your favorite band, the Free Spirits!" This grabs my attention. I actually sit up and look at him. For a moment, I forget all about my problems as I listen to my baby brother telling me about his gig. I am proud of him. I don't remember the last gig his band had.

He tells me all about the venue, how many people are expected to be there, how much the band is getting paid.

"Come on. We are leaving in two hours. I'm not taking no for an answer."

"I'm going. I'm going. You don't need to keep badgering me. When we were kids, I promised that I would go to all of your gigs. So, I am going. Just shut up about it." There's an annoyance in my voice. I sound very aggressive. I hope I don't sound as bad as I think I do. I don't want to ruin Jason's night. I just don't know how to be nice anymore. I feel angry all the time.

I agreed to go. I can't go back on my word.

I can't believe that I actually agreed.

I take a shower and put on some fresh clothes. That is overwhelming and exhausting. I have to take a nap on the couch.

I hope that nobody else in the family goes to his show. I don't think I can handle it.

They take every opportunity to convince me to see a therapist. Seeing the last therapist was a horrible, terrible experience. It was almost as traumatizing as being locked up in the basement. I can't go through that again.

Jason just leaves it alone. He doesn't say anything to me. In fact, he stands up for me. Especially when the discussion turns to the topic of antidepressants.

I refuse to take any drugs.

A part of me feels like I wanted it to happen. Just because I didn't realize the monster was there violating me again and again. That medication took away the little bit of control that I had left.

Never again!

I will not take that chance.

"It's time to leave," Jason says, giving me a nudge.

Anxiety starts to take hold of me. My vision decides to leave. Everything goes black. I can't see anything.

"It's going to be okay, Mandy. Liz and Victor are meeting us there. There will be security there."

"What if he knows and follows us?"

"Then let him! If he's there, I can guarantee you he won't leave the venue alive! I want that bastard dead! I hate what he's done to you!"

That's what I like about Jason. He believes me. He listens to what I say and don't say. He doesn't patronize me. Everybody else would try to convince me that the monster wasn't stalking me. It's been a year, and the monster has moved on, is in prison, or dead. I don't believe that. I'll never be convinced of that.

The few times I have stepped outside, I've felt his gaze. Everybody else would try to convince me that it was all in my head.

We go to the concert. This is the first real gig I've been to of his. The band has some new songs that I've never heard before. I find them inspiring. I've never told Jason this, but it was his music that helped me survive the basement. I don't know. I would try to remember his voice. When we were kids, he would joke how his singing was so bad it even scared monsters away.

I don't really have any fun. I want to. I try to. I am afraid the entire time. I am afraid to let down my guard. I can picture his face when I close my eyes. Is it really his face that I am seeing? I only saw him for a couple of minutes. That was over a year ago.

After the concert, we go to Victor's and Liz's kenpo school. They are throwing a congratulations party for the Free Spirits.

I don't want to be there. I just want to go home. I find myself feeling resentful. Nobody told me about this party. If they had, I wouldn't have gone. I would have broken my promise to Jason. They knew that.

I don't say anything. I don't want to ruin Jason's night.

Instead, I hide in the corner. I have a clear view of the entrances and windows. I can see everybody. There is no way anyone can sneak up on me.

A middle-aged man approaches me. At the same time, he keeps his distance.

"You're Victor's sister, Mandy?"

I nod.

"I'm Ethan. My kids train here. They love it. We've been coming here for about six months now. My kids are constantly talking about this place. Liz was telling me how they're looking for a bigger place. They're outgrowing this space."

He keeps on talking. I'm not sure about what. I feel so vile. I don't understand why anyone would want to talk to me.

"You know," he says, "they're worried about you, Mandy."

"I have to go."

"Okay. Here," He hands me his business card. "I know how overwhelming everything must be, but if you ever want to talk, my office is next door. Or you can email me." He walks away.

I look down at the card. He's a therapist. When I look up, I notice Victor and Liz are watching. A surge of anger races through me. I feel so betrayed. I walk over to them, screaming and yelling. I am causing a major scene, and I didn't care. The whole thing was a setup!

Jason appears out of nowhere.

"Don't be pissed at them. Be mad at me. It was my idea. I knew you would come out for the show. I talked Victor into throwing a party. I asked Ethan to talk to you. He's my therapist. I've been seeing him. I like him. I think you would too. It kills me seeing you like this. I can't handle it. That monster is winning, you know." He has tears in his eyes. His voice cracks a bit as he talks.

I stand there, dumbstruck. There is nothing I can say. Jason is right. I am letting that monster win. I might as well be dead, because I am not living. Right now, I don't care. For some perverse reason, I like seeing Jason like this. He's hurting. I'm glad. I feel like a horrible person. I just want everybody to be hurt. I don't know why.

Monster

I'm getting bored with Twelve. At first, it was satisfying seeing her all disheveled and broken, but now it's boring. I want to move on. I can't. I am not done with her. I will become that monster that she wants me to be. I won't disappoint her.

I'm bored, though.

When I get bored, I drive.

I've been driving aimlessly around for hours. I am not sure where I am. I just know that I'm in some small, quaint town. It reminds me of the town where Twelve used to live, quiet and peaceful.

As I am cruising around, I see somebody who reminds me of Twelve. She is on the sidewalk, jogging. She is tall, athletic, and radiant. She looks like somebody full of confidence.

I wonder if she is a snob or conceited like Twelve.

I roll down the passenger-side window and stop near her.

"Excuse me?" I yell out the window. "Excuse me?"

She stops and looks in my direction.

"Hey there, I'm sorry to bother you. I'm lost. Can you tell me what town this is? I'm looking for Mayville, but I think I took the wrong exit?"

She starts talking. She is so chipper and perky. I'm not listening as she speaks. I'm too busy watching her lips. The way they move as she talks is alluring.

I feel a tinge of excitement. It's been a while. I want her. God, do I ever. I need her to join my collection.

Damn it! I don't have a collection anymore. Twelve took it from me. She took everything from me—the objects, notebooks, John Smith's house. That was the perfect neighborhood to do whatever in. Nobody really cared. They all minded their own business and kept to themselves.

I bid the woman farewell and drive off. I watch her in the rearview mirror. I want her. I need to have her. It's been such a long time.

I check the time and look to see what street I'm on. I know what town I'm in now. I continue my drive. The entire time I am thinking about that woman. God, I want her. I need her.

She reminds me so much of Twelve, except that she doesn't seem like a snob. I find myself thinking of her, the sound of her voice, the way she moved her lips, her body. I can't think of anything else. Her voice sounds like Twelve's. Her body reminds me of Twelve's.

The next day, I drive back to that town, hoping that I will be able to see that jogger again. I have a feeling she keeps to a schedule. I want her.

It doesn't surprise me when I see her jogging. I feel so giddy when I do. She is jogging the same path she did yesterday. It's the same time too.

She reminds me so much of Twelve, both in looks and in personality. I can't help but fantasize about what it would be like to break her. Would she be like the others, easy and boring? Or more like Twelve, infuriating? Or would it be somewhere in between?

I can't wait to get to know her better.

The more I get to know her, the more she reminds me of Twelve. The more I find myself obsessing over her. She consumes my every thought.

I'm going to bring her back to Twelve's old house. She lives three hours away from there. I always go to different towns to collect my objects. I never collect them close by or go to the same town twice. Good thing I love to drive.

I'm not sure what to call this new object. Should I call her One since this is a new game? Should I call her Thirteen since she will be my thirteenth? I'll figure it out, but one thing is for sure: she will become mine. She will call me Lord.

I am so thrilled. I can't wait for this to happen. It's been a while since I have felt this way. I'm flying high now. It's an awesome feeling of euphoria. I feel so powerful. She will know me as Lord. She will call me Lord. All the other objects did— except Twelve, but that is going to change.

I am only collecting Thirteen because she reminds me of Twelve and because I find her inspirational. I now know how to become the monster that Twelve needs me to be.

This isn't about her; it's about Twelve. I'm thinking of skipping most of that first stage, the getting-to-know-each-other stage, because it really isn't about Thirteen.

I need to be a bit more discreet about this since I am taking this object to an affluent neighborhood. I normally just bludgeon the object into submission. That neighborhood where Twelve used to live, everybody has become so much more vigilant.

They still talk about it.

The day Twelve disappeared, they act as if it happened yesterday. For whatever reason, they love talking to me about it. Maybe it's because I'm the newcomer. If only they knew. It makes my day talking to them. They are clueless, just like the police. It makes me feel in control and powerful.

This is going to be a new game with new rules. I need to figure out how to roofie her. That's the best way to collect her. This is going to be wonderful. She is so much like Twelve. I wonder if she has the same touch, feel, and smell as Twelve.

I need her, Thirteen. From now on, that will be her new name. Her regular name will no longer exist. Thirteen. After all, she will be my thirteenth object. I have followed Thirteen around enough to understand what her routine is. I know where she lives, where she works, and what she likes to do in her spare time.

Collecting her shouldn't be a problem. The only problem now is making the preparations. I will bring her back to

Twelve's old house. I think that will be romantic, completing the circle. Twelve should appreciate the symbolism in this.

That house needs some renovations. It's in fantastic shape. I just need to add some soundproofing and see if I can make a basement. It's a split-level. You come in the front door, and there is one level. Near the kitchen is a staircase that goes downstairs and one that goes upstairs.

There isn't a wall or a door. I'm going to see if I can get one of my neighbors to help.

He's a construction worker. I want there to be a wall. I want to be able to open up a door to go downstairs. I want to be able to keep the objects there and lock the door so they can't escape. The downstairs doesn't have any windows, so it's perfect.

I am so excited about starting this new endeavor. I haven't been able to sleep. I just can't wait. It's going to be ideal. It has to be. Twelve deserves the best and nothing less.

It takes me a couple of months to get the house up to par. I spend all my free time working on the house and visiting Thirteen. I can't wait for her to become mine.

Twelve

I can't believe I actually allowed Jason to convince me to go out. It was scary as hell. The entire time, I was convinced that the monster would just magically appear. He didn't. I don't want to go back out ever again. I don't want to give him that opportunity.

That was a few days ago. I'm still pissed at Jason. It feels like the whole thing was a ruse. I know that the gig wasn't, but everything that happened afterward was.

He set me up to meet a therapist.

I feel betrayed by him. Jason was the only person who didn't badger me about going back to therapy. He knew why I didn't want to try it again.

He never pretended that my kidnapping didn't happen. He just never talked about it. He asked me to get help once when he saw that I was drowning.

I appreciate that. I told him that I couldn't, and I gave him reasons why. He seemed to understand.

Then he had to go and do this.

It has me so pissed off. It's something that I would expect from Victor or our parents, but not him.

It's early morning. It must be. I'm hungry. I feel the need to leave my little room. I am ready to interact with another person if I have to. However, nobody should be around. Parents should be at work. I haven't seen Jason since his gig, and Meghan should still be sleeping at this time.

I feel pretty confident that it is safe to go down to the kitchen and not see a single person. I pray that the kitchen and the path to the kitchen is empty. I don't want to talk to anybody. I don't want anybody to talk to me.

As I walk into the kitchen, I see Jason. I wasn't expecting to see him. I'm so mad at him. He's the last person that I want to see.

"Hey, Mandy!" he says when he sees me. His usual smile is not there. His voice sounds serious. I don't hear that hint of humor in it.

"I'm not talking to you," I say as I turn to leave.

"I know, but we need to talk." He grabs my shoulder. I turn around, ready to slug him across the face. He really is on my last nerve.

"I've been so worried about you, Mandy. We all are. Well, I can't do this anymore. I can't sit here, watching you throw your life away, and pretend that all is fine. It's not. It's far from it. You have to start living again. You have to find a way to start living again."

"You know what? Screw you, Jason! You have no idea what the hell's going on! I'm so sick and tired of everybody telling me what I should or should not be doing. I am a goddamn adult. I wish everybody would start treating me as such."

"Then act like one! Instead of a moody intolerable teenager. You're right, I have no idea what's going on with you because you don't talk. You don't talk to me, you don't talk to anybody. You have shut completely down. You have stopped living."

"He's still out there! How the hell do you expect me to get on with my life when he is out there somewhere? He is not done with me yet. That's what he kept saying. He has something special for me planned. I will start living again once that bastard is caught or, better yet, is dead. Either way, he needs to be completely out of the picture. Everything will be better then. So, do me a favor. Just leave me alone until then!"

"No! I can't do that. Not anymore. Think about it, Mandy: what if that monster is never caught? Then what? Are you just going to waste away until you die? Don't you see this is what he wants? You are playing right into him. What about VJ? He doesn't understand. The only thing VJ knows is that you were there with him every single day of his life. Then you went away for a very long time. Then you came back and didn't want anything to do with him. That has him so upset. He doesn't understand why you don't love him anymore. It's the only thing he talks about. You know he loves you more than he loves his own parents. Victor and Liz were always jealous about it. And Maria is just mad that you are no longer there. Look, all I am asking is for you to contact Ethan. Call him, shoot him an email, or find somebody else to talk to. I don't care. The point is you need to do something to help yourself. Right now, this monster is winning. Wherever he is, he has all this power and control over you. Don't give him that power. You have to gain control. Don't let him win. Please, don't let him win. You can't."

I stand there in the kitchen, gawking at Jason. I don't know what to say or do. I feel like a total and complete idiot. He's made some good points. It's just I am so scared. I don't know what to do. I feel so frozen that I can't move most days.

When I try, it's like there is this invisible hand choking the life out of me. It only loosens its grip when I step back in time. I can't move on. It doesn't allow it.

It really irks me, though. Jason has always been the fun one. He always has a joke or two. He never takes anything seriously. I don't ever remember him having a serious conversation with anybody in my life. "Serious" is one word that isn't in his vocabulary. Until now.

Everything he said strikes a chord with me. I'm sure that over the course of the last year, my parents, or Victor have said the same thing to me. I just never heard it. With Jason, I hear every word.

I stand there, dumbfounded.

"Just think about what I said. Okay, Mandy? I have to go."

I watch Jason leave the house.

"You know, he's right."

I jump at the sound of Meghan's voice. I didn't realize somebody else was in the kitchen with us. I turn to face her.

"Oh, not you too," I grumble out.

I go to leave the kitchen, but Meghan blocks my way.

"Get out of my way! I'm going to hit you if you don't! Just get out of my damn way!" I say through gritted teeth. I have this urge to destroy everything in sight.

"No. Mandy. No. Little brother is right. It's not often I say that, but he is. Not that you will listen to anybody anyways because you are so selfish and conceited like that."

"Meghan, shut up. I don't like you and never have. So, stop wasting my time."

"And I can't stand you. Do you even realize how insufferable you are? It's so annoying babysitting Maria and VJ. All they want is you. And you don't even care. That's the worst part. You don't care. You don't care about anything. It just seems that you have forgotten how to care. You have lost interest in everything and everyone. It's a shame. You are allowing him to win, and you don't even know it. Or maybe you do? Maybe you want him to win? It's easier that way, right? At least you survived."

People keep telling me that at least I survived—if that is what you want to call it. I'm always afraid, jumping at every sound. I don't want to close my eyes. Every time I blink, I see him lingering over me. I'm terrified of other people. I just want to be left alone.

I will never be alone. I can always feel the man in me. I shudder at the thought. He only shows his face in the darkness.

I really hate to admit it, but Meghan is right. I will never tell her that, though.

I have lost interest in everything that has made me me. My family has always been the most important part of my life. We were always so close. Even now, as adults, we go on vacation together.

When I was locked in that basement, it was the thought of seeing my family that kept me going. I swear they were what kept me alive. I dreamt of seeing them again, especially Maria and VJ.

Now, I can't even tell you the first thing about them. I can't even tell you the first thing about me. I have lost touch with reality and my family. I don't know the last time I saw VJ or Maria. I feel so disconnected from the world. I feel so alone. I'm so lost. I'm scared.

I take a deep breath and hold it because, right now, I just want to beat up Meghan. I have this need to make her hurt. It doesn't make sense to me why I want everybody around me to hurt. I just do. Misery loves company, right. I exhale. I'm trying to be civil, but I'm not sure if I can.

"Where are you going anyway? It's, like, six in the morning," I ask, realizing Meghan has a purse in one hand and car keys in the other.

"Wow! Try four thirty in the afternoon. I'm going out. Probably to a bar someplace. I didn't really think about it. I just don't want to be here when Mom and Dad come back from work."

"Why? What happened? What's going on?"

"Ahh, look at you, pretending to care. Come along, and I will tell you. You're buying."

"What the…? I have no money."

"Hey, it's not my fault that you're a freeloader. Miss Too-perfect-to-work." Meghan winks at me. She looks down at her watch.

"Come on," she says. "I have a better idea."

She grabs my hand and starts leading me to the door.

"Where are we going?" I ask. It never occurs to me that we might actually be going someplace. The only time we can manage to act civil toward one another is at family functions, and even then, our conversations turn into altercations.

"The dojo. Didn't you know Maria and VJ are taking classes now? By the time we get there, the kids' class should be finishing up. We can take them out to dinner. We just have to make sure Victor or Liz gives us the money. And with you there, how can they possibly say no?"

Together, Meghan and I leave the house. It never occurs to me that I am actually leaving, though. We are halfway to the school when I realize we are no longer at home. I start freaking out, having a total one hundred percent anxiety attack.

It is scary.

We pull up to the school.

"Hey," Meghan says, "do your best to have fun. I know it scares you, but you are not alone."

We walk into the school.

The look on little VJ's face when he sees me is priceless. He does a double take. He then plows right into me, knocking me over with his hugs.

I have only seen him once in the past year. He has grown so much. Maria doesn't look happy to see me. She has called me several times over the past year. I just couldn't bring myself to talk to her. It wasn't her. It was everybody: friends, family, neighbors, and ex-coworkers. I ignored them all.

Maria took it personally. She's a kid; I expected her to. Yet I couldn't actually bring myself to talk to her.

Liz takes all of us out to dinner.

I jump at every sound. I'm generally all shaky. It's very difficult holding silverware. This has become my norm.

VJ is so excited that he is talking a mile a minute. He started preschool. He is telling me all about that. He really loves his teacher. He is telling me about his new friends that he met there. He is telling me about all of his new toys. He is now a yellow belt in Kenpo. He tells me how much he loves training. He shows me his new smartwatch. Maria has one too. He can play games on it, it has a video camera on it, and you can record and send messages. It also has a built-in GPS so parents know where their kids are. I don't think VJ understands a word he is saying. He's just excited that the watch face is a Star Wars stormtrooper. Maria's smartwatch has the same functions, but it's Hello Kitty.

Maria is being so quiet. I try getting her to talk to me. She just won't. Even Liz is trying to get her to talk to me. Maria just rolls her eyes.

Near the end of dinner, she finally speaks.

"Aunt Mandy, you're an idiot. How come everybody else, even a kid, can see that you are not well, but yet you can't even see it in your own self? I don't like this you. I hope it's not going to be the new you. I want the old you back. Please do whatever you can to get that old you back. Please. Promise me that."

I start bawling my eyes out. Right in the middle of the restaurant. It's so embarrassing. I can't stop crying.

"Mom, can we leave now? I don't want to be here."

"Maria, I promise. I promise," I tell her as she leaves the table with VJ and Liz.

Monster

After I'm done with the home improvements, I go back to where Thirteen lives. It's been a while since I have seen her. I spend a few days getting reacquainted with her. She is as marvelous as I remember.

Just like Twelve, she is also a creature of habit. She goes out for a jog at the same exact time every day. She follows the same route every single day. Before her jog, she always opens up a bottle of Gatorade and puts it in the fridge. After she finishes jogging, she goes straight for that open bottle of Gatorade.

On one of Thirteen's runs, I sneak into her house. I want to surprise her. I slip a little something something into her open bottle of Gatorade. I put it back in the fridge. I hide in a coat closet in the kitchen and wait. She should return soon. My heart is racing. I can't wait for her to become mine.

Thirteen.

She will be mine. She will call me Lord.

About ten minutes later, she is in the house. I hear her opening up the refrigerator. I have the closet door opened slightly. I peer out, watching everything that she is doing. As I knew she would, she goes for that bottle of Gatorade in the fridge and guzzles it down. Good. It shouldn't take long now. Soon, she will be mine.

I wait a minute before coming out of the closet.

"Hi there!" I say. She jumps and turns around, dropping the partially finished Gatorade. "Hi, Thirteen! Do you remember me? We met a few months back. My name is Lord."

She looks scared and confused, but she doesn't say anything. I chuckle. She reminds me so much of Twelve. It's wonderful.

"Why don't you sit down before you get hurt?" I ask her. She is swaying unsteadily on her feet. I can tell that the roofie has kicked in.

I quickly grab her arm. She is close to toppling over. I guide her to a nearby chair.

"It's okay," I whisper into her ear. "I got you."

I give her a second; my hand is still on her arm. She doesn't say anything, she doesn't move, and she doesn't fight back.

I leave her for a minute as I go and grab another one of her Gatorade. I open it and put something special in it. I'm not sure how long the effects will last. It's a long drive back to Twelve's old house. I bring the extra bottle just in case.

"Come on. Get up," I command Thirteen as I help her to her feet. I guide her out of her house and into my car. She doesn't fight. She does everything I tell her to do. It's nice getting her into my car without having any struggle.

We drive back to Twelve's old house.

It's a long drive back.

The entire drive, I think about Twelve. I haven't seen her in a while. Not since I discovered Thirteen. It's been a few months. I hope she's still with her parents. I hope that I haven't missed too much of her life. Somehow, I don't think I have.

I imagine her being as disheveled as ever. That's okay if she is. It will give me time to execute my plan.

The drive back to the house seems to take forever. I swear it's taking longer than the three hours that it normally does. Maybe it's because I am excited.

I can't wait to get there.

I can't wait for the fun that Thirteen and I are going to have. I do sincerely hope she feels like Twelve. Almost everything else about her is similar to Twelve, including her smell. Oh, I can't wait. It's so exciting. It gives me a buzz.

I love having that power and control. She will know me as Lord. I am going to make sure of that. In this extremely chaotic world, I'm in complete control when I am with my objects.

That's one of the only times I feel at peace. I am so relaxed when I am with them. I can feel all of my stress just oozing away. It is a great feeling.

I do miss that feeling. Hopefully, Thirteen will help alleviate the stress. It's been too long.

I miss my notebooks. They helped to relieve some of the stress in between objects. Without those journals, I am stressed. I feel like I am losing control. There is no worse feeling than that of not being in control.

The entire ride back to the house, Thirteen is in a stupor. She doesn't say anything. She doesn't move. She seems to be in a peaceful sleep.

It's a three-hour ride. We are almost at the house. How much did I give her? I hope it wasn't too much. I drugged her with my own special concoction. I got the drugs from work. I am a part-time drug rep. I can make my own hours. I can work as many hours as I want or don't want. I love having that freedom.

We pull into the driveway, and Thirteen is still out of it. I get out of the car and open up the passenger-side door. I help her out of my car. She is in a suggestible state of mind.

She can't move on her own accord. If I command her to get up, she will, but I have to guide her a little. She walks on her own with a little guidance from me. It makes it much easier getting her into the house, especially with these neighbors. After the incident, they feel the need to be nosy. It's annoying but understandable.

I take Thirteen down to the basement. I can't wait. This is so exciting! I feel like a little kid at a candy store.

I can feel the stress of the past year catching up to me. I'm feeling it physically, emotionally, and spiritually. Thirteen should be a good outlet for all that stress. She looks so beautiful right now, lying on the floor.

I start to remove her clothes. My heart is fluttering in my chest. I can't wait to touch her. She should feel like Twelve.

Everything else about her reminds me of Twelve. I wonder if her skin will too.

Thirteen tries to fight back.

"Shhh, just relax and enjoy it. Let me do all the work," I whisper reassuringly as I use my knee to spread her legs apart.

I use my left hand to explore her body.

The entire time, Thirteen whimpers incoherently, and she does her best to fight and resist me. I find that surprising, as she is still in a drug-induced state of mind.

It is one of the greatest feelings in the world, having her squirm underneath me.

She's not exactly like Twelve, as I thought. I find that disappointing. I thought she would make an excellent substitute.

I finish up with Thirteen. It's good but disappointing. She just isn't Twelve. Twelve is the best. I can't wait for her to become mine again. She is all I can think about every second of every day.

I dream about her constantly. No matter what I do and what I try, I cannot get Twelve out of my head. It's frustrating. I need her. Even when I am with Thirteen, all I can think about is Twelve.

The drugs in Thirteen are wearing off. She is becoming aggressive and loud. Extremely loud! She's screaming for help. I don't understand why. She wanted this to happen. If she didn't, she wouldn't have stopped to talk to me. It's that simple. She wanted me.

I know she enjoyed it.

I wonder if she is having regrets about it now.

I do my best to calm her down. My attempts are feeble. I hoped she would be more like Twelve.

Thirteen is sitting on the floor. She looks loopy. She is yelling, screaming, hollering for help. I hope that nobody can hear her.

I'm holding her shoulder, talking to her soothingly. Her back is against the wall when she turns and clobbers me in the jaw with her elbow. I nearly bite my tongue, my teeth chattering. I fall backward.

She scrambles away from me. She is trying to get on her feet, but she can't seem to find her balance. She isn't far from me. I'm able to reach out and grab her ankle. She falls. I crawl on top of her, straddling her. She is still fighting with all of her energy. I grab her head and hit it against the floor until she stops.

She loses consciousness.

I go upstairs. I grab the spiked Gatorade and a bottle of aspirin. I am rummaging through the rooms, looking for rope, wire, or even duct tape. Something to tie her up with. In my excitement, I forgot to make sure that I had something that I could use to restrain her with.

I go back down to the basement. She is still unconscious. I watch her. I pretend she is Twelve at John Smith's house.

Those days were perfect. I wonder if Twelve thinks about me as much as I think about her. I hope so. She was perfect. Life will be perfect again once I have her. Sure, we had our problems—that was part of the charm.

I don't know how long I've been watching Thirteen and reminiscing about Twelve, but she finally starts to stir a little. She moans. Her hand goes straight up to her head.

"Are you okay?" I ask her. She looks at me, rolls over on her side, and throws up.

"Do you need something to wash your mouth out with?" I ask. She just looks at me, blinking. She is still dazed and doesn't say anything.

"Hey, I'm sincerely sorry about your head. I didn't mean to get rough with you. In all fairness, you were the one that attacked me. I was only defending myself. You must have a killer headache, eh? Here, take these. They will help with your head." I open up the Gatorade for her and hand it to her along with the aspirin.

She refuses to take them. I smile. This brings back fond memories of Twelve.

"Come on. Take it. It's just aspirin."

"You're fucking crazy! Please just let me go."

I find myself smiling at her. Right now, she is being an exact replica of Twelve. I gently touch her lips with my hand. She swats my hand away. I graze her breast. I don't think she realized I had taken off her clothes until then. She starts freaking out, calling me all types of obscene names. I keep telling her my name is Lord and not the others, but she keeps insisting on calling me.

"Come on, just take the aspirin. It should help take the edge off. I imagine that you have a killer headache. I am just trying to help. I am not going to hurt you."

I'm standing close to her. I can feel the heat radiating off her body. She doesn't take the aspirin or Gatorade. Instead, she spits in my face. God, I just want to hit her. I can't believe how disrespectful she is being. I clean the spit off my face.

"What do you want with me? Why am I here?" she sobs out.

"I'll answer all your questions on one condition. Take the aspirin. Please. I just might let you go if you do. If you don't obey me, you will never leave this place. The choice is yours."

Very grudgingly, she takes the pills and washes them down with the laced Gatorade.

"Now, what are your questions again?" I ask her.

She tries to answer, slurring her words slightly before passing out.

I figure I have about four hours to visit Twelve. I haven't seen her in months. I also need to buy some type of wire to bind Thirteen with. I thought I had something at the house and didn't double-check to make sure.

I should be fine with the drugs in her system.

I just need to visit Twelve. I haven't seen her in ages. I miss her. I need her. I make it to Twelve's parents' house. It's dark outside. I am surprised to see her leaving with her twin.

Twelve gets into the passenger side of the car, and her sister is on the driver's side. They drive off.

I follow.

They go to a karate school. They're there for about twenty minutes. They pick up two kids and a woman. It's dark out. I can't see who they are. I think the kids are Twelve's niece and nephew. They go to a restaurant.

Twelve jumps at every sound. It's a pleasant surprise seeing her out and about. God, I want her. I need her. To touch her again would be bliss. I can't wait for her to be mine. I miss her so much. I never felt this way with the other objects.

Shit!

Time is almost up. I still need something to tie Thirteen up with. I do the hardest thing ever and drag myself away from Twelve. It's a euphoric feeling, sitting in the restaurant without her even knowing it. I was also hiding up at the bar. I didn't want to take any chances. Right now, though, I have Thirteen to tend to. I have to go.

I go back to the house. First thing I do is check on Thirteen. She is still pretty out of it. I go to the neighbor's house across the street. I ask him if he has duct tape. I am delighted that he does. I go back to the house and tape Thirteen's hands together.

Twelve

I can't believe I went out again. I don't know how I let Meghan convince me in the first place. We normally don't hang out together. Period. At the restaurant, I swear I saw him. He is always with me, though. Everywhere I turn, I swear he is there. Not only do I see him every now and again, but I can smell him. He has a very distinct odor: stale cigarettes, cologne, and gin.

I mention this to Meghan and Liz, and of course, they think I am being paranoid. I don't believe them. The man kept telling me that I was extremely special and that, because I was special, he had something extraordinary planned for me. I know he was the one who made that anonymous tip. He was the only one who knew where I was. Even when I was rescued, he would break into my house to violate me over and over again. I am still nauseated by it.

I can't really enjoy being out. I want to. I try so hard to have a good time. I can't, though. It's just too scary. I'm in constant panic mode. It always feels like I am having an asthma attack. I can't breathe. I can't stop shaking. I feel lightheaded and dizzy all the time.

It's nice seeing the kids, though. Maria broke my heart. I'm not mad at her. She was only being honest. She doesn't want to see me until I'm better.

Because of her, I sent Ethan an email. It took me several days to compose it. I need to start doing something instead of wasting away. My baby brother is right, I can't wait for the monster to be captured. If he never is, I will never start living. The monster will win.

It's hard. I know he is out there. I'm just waiting for his next move. There are times, especially at night, that I wish I were dead. The only reason I haven't killed myself is because I don't want the monster to win.

I think about the basement and its cold cement floor. I had duct tape covering my eyes for weeks. I remember the paramedics. I heard them talking in my semi-conscious state. Nothing they said made sense. I thought I was dead, but I do remember one paramedic telling somebody not to remove the tape because there was a chance my skin would come off with it.

It scares me to think about that now. The coldness and the darkness are what I remember the most. It is so real. It's all I think about. I can't think of anything else. I am trapped in that darkness. There is no escape.

It's all I think about, but I can't bring myself to talk about it. It's too embarrassing. It's too degrading. I feel so ashamed of myself. I know these feelings are misguided, but I can't help but feel this way.

Ethan responds to my email. I can't bring myself to read it or to respond to it. So, I ignore it.

I have had such crappy experiences with therapists. I am afraid to repeat them. In my mind, I am not breaking my promise to Maria.

I discover that I roam around the house more. I see my siblings gathering around the kitchen. They stop talking the moment I enter the room.

"Welcome to the best water hole in the house!" Jason exclaims. I laugh. It surprises me. I thought I'd forgotten how to laugh. It's been such a long time.

"So…" Jason says, clapping me on the shoulder, "I had my appointment with Ethan today. He told me that you emailed him but haven't responded back to his reply."

"Yeah, I didn't realize he had responded. I haven't checked my email," I say, lying. I don't want to tell Jason the truth with Victor right there. I don't want Maria to accidentally find out that I am not doing everything in my power to help myself. I am doing what I can, though.

I want to see her. I miss her. I miss VJ.

"That was a nice surprise yesterday. The kids loved seeing you, even Maria. Liz told me what she said. VJ wants to see you again. He misses you," Victor says.

I don't know what to say. I just nod.

"We were just discussing this. We're thinking of letting Mom and Dad watch VJ for the weekend. I just wanted to run that by you first. He will bug the hell out of you. I just want to make sure you are cool with it first."

"Yeah, I know that I have a tendency to snap at anybody who looks at me the wrong way or breathes too loudly. I'm working on it."

"That's right! You and Meghan have been in the same room for five minutes now, and no catfight," Jason says jokingly. He's right, though. Meghan and I have never been able to spend more than five minutes with each other before having some type of altercation break out.

"I would like to see the little guy. I miss him so much. I need some normalcy. Will Maria be here too?" I ask Victor.

"No, it's her best friend's birthday. She will be there."

***

VJ stayed with us for the weekend. He is four. Right now, his favorite thing is to sneak up on people, jump out in front of them, and yell, "BOO!" He then goes into his laughing fits. For whatever reason, he finds this hilarious. That's my VJ.

Nobody warned me about that.

He did this to me, and I did the worst thing possible. I slugged him across the face. Hard.

I felt so horrible.

I didn't know it was him. I didn't realize it. I should have, but my mind plays tricks on me. I thought it was that monster. I really did. I was just trying to defend myself.

Once I heard the little boy cry, it brought me back to reality. I couldn't believe what I had done. I didn't remember doing it. At the same time, I did remember. I became scared of myself.

I love that boy to death. When VJ was an infant and would cry, all I needed to do was to touch his arm, and he would stop. It didn't matter what type of mood he was in. All I needed to do was to hold him, and he would get this big goofy smile on his face. He always smiled when I was around.

We definitely had a bond. When VJ became older, he would tell everybody who would listen to him how I was his favorite person—other than mommy and daddy, of course.

And I hit him.

I hit him. I feel like such a monster.

The moment I realized what I had done, I turned on my heels and ran out the back door. I bolted away from the house. It was the first time I'd left the house on my own since I'd been rescued. For a brief flicker in time, I forgot all about the man.

My parents were there. They saw the whole thing, from when VJ snuck up on me and then my reaction. My mom went over to VJ, and my dad ran out of the house after me.

"Mandy! Mandy!"

I ignored him.

I ignored everything around me. Instead of being in a place that I'd grown up in and a town that I knew quite well, I was in that cellar. For a moment, I really thought I was in that basement again. I gagged from the smell: feces, vomit, blood, gin, cigarettes, and cologne—I will never forget it. I may no longer be in that basement, but I did become a prisoner in my own mind.

I was a block away from the house when I collapsed to my knees, crying hysterically.

I could hear my dad right behind me. "Mandy?"

It's weird; I knew it was my dad who stood behind me and whispered my name. In my mind, though, it was the monster. But then I knew that couldn't be right, because my name isn't Mandy. It's Twelve.

I feel like I'm losing my freaking mind!

"I wish I was dead!" I sobbed out. That's the first time I told anybody my secret. It isn't that I want to die; I just don't want to live. The pain is too much. It's too overwhelming. I can't bear it anymore. I doubt it will ever go away. It just gets worse, day after day.

"Why didn't he kill me? I wish that he had. Why didn't he? He killed eleven women. Eleven women! Why did he let me go?"

"I don't know. I don't know." My dad's voice was nothing more than a whisper. He knelt down next to me. "I wish I had answers for you, kiddo, but I don't."

"I hit VJ. I hit him! How could I just hit a little kid like that? Only monsters do that."

"You're not a monster, kiddo. You're anything but."

I could tell that my dad wanted to put his arm around my shoulder and hold me, like he would when I was a little girl and was scared about something. Now, I can't stand it when somebody touches me.

"VJ's going to hate me. Liz and Victor are going to kill me."

"No, they're not. They love you. They understand."

"How can they understand? Nobody freaking knows or understands what I went through!" I was lashing out, but I didn't care. At that moment, all I wanted was to throw a hissy fit, and I tried to think of something horrible to say to my dad.

His mere presence was making me angry. He was being so nice and understanding. I just wanted him to hurt as much as I do.

"You're right," he said sternly.

I hadn't heard that tone in my father's voice since I was a teenager. As a kid, I'd done my best not to listen to my parents, but every time he would get that tone in his voice, I couldn't help but listen. I hated that tone.

For a moment, I stopped crying. For the first time in a year, I'd actually heard my dad when he'd spoken. He'd finally brought me out of my own head.

"You're right," he continued, "I can't imagine the hell that you are living. I am so sorry that had to happen to you. I can only imagine that it completely shattered any belief you may have about the world being a safe place. I don't know what to say. Or how to comfort you. I am so sorry that you had to go through that, but you don't have to go through it alone. I am here. We are all here. I want to help. Just let me help. We all want to help you. All you need to do is let us."

I looked up at my dad. I hadn't realized that I'd been pushing him—and everybody else, for that matter—away. I'd been doing my best to push everyone out of my life. I saw myself doing it, but I didn't realize I was doing it. I guess it was my way of punishing myself. I really don't know.

I hugged him. We sat there, hugging each other and crying, until there were no more tears.

"Anyway," he said, winking at me, "who would spoil that child if not you? VJ has you wrapped around his little pinkie. He could never stay mad at you just because you're the only one who does spoil him, and he knows it."

The walk home seemed like the longest walk ever. I enjoyed the warmth of the sun. I didn't want the sun to disappear. I was afraid that I would never see it again. It was the only thing that soothed the aches and eased the pain. I took a deep breath and tried to relax, but I became anxious as the dread of the night approached.

The first thing I did when we got home was apologize to VJ. He seemed to have forgotten all about it. I then read and replied to the email Ethan had sent me. I was nervous as hell about setting up an appointment. I had to. I didn't want something like this to happen again. I couldn't let it happen again.

I'm tired of hating myself. I'm tired of wanting to be dead and being bitterly disappointed when I wake up and know that I'm still alive.

Monster

I'm getting bored with Thirteen. She just isn't Twelve. In so many ways, she isn't. She doesn't fight back anymore. That's disappointing. I need her to, but she doesn't. She disobeys me whenever she can.

"If you're going to kill me, then kill me. I'm done indulging you," she says to me one night. I had smacked her across the face. I was trying to get her to scream for me. I needed her to, but she wouldn't.

I make sure she is securely tied. I drug her again, forcing her to swallow the laced water. I don't want to take any chances. Somebody might hear her if she starts screaming.

I walk out of the basement. I turn the stereo in the living room on. I leave the house. I need to see Twelve. I feel like my world is unraveling without her. I know she wants me. We have a connection. There's a spark between us. I'm doing my best to keep it alive.

As I'm driving around, I see a girl. She lives in the same neighborhood as Twelve and her parents.

The girl isn't my type. She is a little too young. I want her, though. I know the girl doesn't interact with Twelve. Nobody does. The girl does know the family. I see her walking with Twelve's younger brother. They're talking.

I learn where the girl lives. I go back home. The entire time, I am thinking about the girl. She has a familiarity with Twelve.

I want her. She can help me stay connected to Twelve.

The next day, I decide to follow the girl, learning as much as I can about her. The girl's name is Summer. She's a sophomore in high school. She loves dogs. She owns a cute chocolate Lab. That's all I know about her. I only know that much because I have a familiarity with everyone who is associated with Twelve and her family. I follow her for a few days. I need to know her routine and her parents.

I'm cruising down the street in a white Honda CRV. My ride looks like every other ride in suburbia. I'm a few houses away from Summer's house. She is at school, and her parents are at work. I park the SUV and get out. I walk to the back of Summer's house.

I don't even realize that I am breaking into her house until it is done. I'm thinking about it—I want to get her dog—but I don't realize that I am actually doing it until her chocolate Lab comes running up to me. He isn't snarling or anything. He's wagging his tale like he's happy to see me. I'm starting to understand why people love dogs.

The Lab is not much of a guard dog, but he is a cute little fellow. It's a lot easier to get him than I anticipated. I carry him out of the house, and the entire time, he's licking my face. We go back to the Honda and wait.

Summer's bus stop is at the corner. She has to pass me to get to her house. I'm going to be on the sidewalk in front of my vehicle with her chocolate Lab when she gets off the bus. The bus should be dropping her off any minute now.

I give the dog some more Beggin' Strips, and then I take him out of the Honda. I leave the passenger-side door wide open. He's sitting on the sidewalk, and I'm kneeling down, patting him. He is a dumb little guy, but he's friendly enough. He will serve a purpose.

I hear the bus screeching to a stop behind me. I hear the talking and laughing of the kids as they descend from the bus.

It's time.

"Hey there, fella," I say to the dog, speaking louder than normal. I want to make sure that Summer is able to hear me. I need to get her attention.

"What are doing out here all by yourself, huh?" I glance behind me and see Summer hurrying in our direction. My heart jumps with joy, a feeling I haven't felt for a couple weeks.

"Where do you live, boy? Your owner must be awfully worried about you."

"Hey! Hey, what the hell are you doing with my dog?"

It's hard not to smile. I have her. Not yet, though.

"This is your dog?" I say, standing up. He is sitting on the sidewalk, wagging his tail wildly as he sees Summer. "I was just driving down the road when I saw him running loose. I didn't want anything bad to happen to him. I was just trying to figure out who he belongs to."

"Oh, um…well, thanks. C'mere, Coco. C'mon, boy." She drops down to her knees and claps her hands.

The dog runs over to her and jumps up to into her arms, making her fall over. His front two paws are on her shoulders, pinning her down as he slobbers all over her face.

I smile. I can't help it.

Summer stands up, laughing.

"That's my good boy," she says, giving the dog a pat on the head.

She stands in front of the Honda, unaware that the passenger door is wide open.

"Coco, is it?"

"Yeah, I've had him since he was just six weeks old. He's my best friend."

"Well, he's a well-behaved fella. Aren't you, boy?"

"He is. I'm just wondering how he got out of the house."

"I don't know. Unfortunately, it happens."

I step closer to her and Coco. I pat Coco on the head. Summer is facing me. Her back is towards the Honda.

I'm standing so close to her that I can smell the shampoo in her hair. I keep talking and patting the dog, and then I look up and smile at Summer.

"What?" she says, taking an uneasy step back.

"Nothing. It's just been a long time."

I grab her arms with my left hand and pull her into me. With my right hand, I grab an airsoft gun from my waistband.

I loathe guns. I always have. I don't own one. I never have, and I don't plan on ever owning one.

I'm taking a gamble, hoping that Summer won't know the difference between a regular gun and an airsoft.

"If you make so much as a peep, I will shoot. Understand?"

She nods. There's that look of mortal terror in her eyes. That's a good, sexy look on a woman. Every time I see that look, I feel like I can fly. It's that inebriating.

"What about Coco?" Her voice is assertive, nothing like I expect.

"What…? Leave him here."

"I can't do that. What if he gets it by a car?"

"I can shoot him now. That way, you don't have to worry about him getting hit by a car. I point the gun at the dumb, cute chocolate Lab."

"NO! I'll go with you." She slides inside the car.

"That's a good girl. Now, give me your cell phone."

"What?"

"Give me your cell phone, or I will put a bullet through your skull," I say, slowly enunciating each word.

She gives me her phone.

I glance around. People are walking on the other side of the street. I smile, trying to act normal. They shouldn't be able to see the gun in my hand. They can't hear our conversation.

I drop her phone on the asphalt and stomp on it. I hurry around to the driver's side of the car, and then I put the key in the ignition and drive like hell out of there. I keep the airsoft trained on Summer. It takes two hours to get back to Twelve's old place; I just want to make sure that nobody is following us.

The entire time, I find myself thinking about Coco. I'm kind of fond of that little guy. He was just so loving and trusting. I don't want anything bad to happen to him. I almost brought the dog with us. That might have made things complicated, though.

There were people around to witness the abduction, mostly teens. Hopefully, I was able to play it off. If they were actually paying attention to us, it should have looked like Summer went with me willingly.

The abduction isn't going as I planned. Summer is proving to be more troublesome than I originally imagined. She won't shut up. I keep threatening to shoot her. A couple of times, she's tried to get out of the car, but I have the doors locked. She is getting on my nerves. I can tell that she is trying to formulate an escape plan.

I pull the car to the side of the road. I check the mirrors. I don't see anybody on the road. I say something to Summer, but she is being so defiant. I smack her on the head with the butt of the airsoft. Now she starts listening to me. I hit a couple more times just because my patience is waning. I don't have time for this. I take her to Twelve's old house. We walk in together. She has some blood on her forehead, but she is actually doing what I tell her to. I hope that none of the neighbors see us. They shouldn't. They should be at work. I use fishing wire to bind Summer's hands and feet.

I carry her down to the basement. I tie her securely up against one of the support beams.

"Your name is Fourteen. It is no longer Summer. You are not a person, but an object. You will know me as Lord. I am almighty and powerful. I have complete control over you now," I tell her as I gently caress her face. Her skin is so soft, much softer than Twelve's. I slowly remove her clothes, savoring it. She's crying and fighting as much as she can.

"You're going to love what I have planned for you," I whisper into her ear. I nibble on her earlobe.

"Get away from her! She's only a child, you fucking psycho!" Thirteen screams in the background. I stop. I can't help but smile.

"Do whatever you want with me. Just don't touch her. I will play your game. Just don't hurt her."

It catches me off guard how she is trying to protect Fourteen. Why would she do that? We live in a world where nobody cares about another person. I remember how, as a kid, I would always try to protect my mother against the abusive men in her life. That would upset her. She didn't want me to help her or protect her. At times, these men smacked me around. My mother did nothing about it. Why would she? She never cared. There were times she would hit me too.

Thirteen refuses to call me Lord. I'm all-powerful and mighty, yet she defies me. She no longer fights back. Just like Twelve.

So, this little outburst of hers surprises me.

I'm not sure what I was hoping for when I collected the younger object. I definitely wasn't expecting Thirteen to sacrifice herself to protect her.

Of course! I should have thought of this sooner. Why didn't I? It would have saved me a lot of trouble and aggravation.

Twelve and I could be living happily ever after instead of not being able to be with each other.

That's how I'm going to break Twelve. Her family is the most important aspect of her life. I knew that. That's the first thing I learned about her in our get-to-know-each-other phase. She had family photos all over her house. They always went on trips together. It was sickening.

When I had listening devices in her house, all she talked about was her family. Her family is her Achilles heel. It's the only way to have Twelve acknowledge me as Lord.

"Fourteen, we are going to have to do this later," I whisper to her. I stand up and go over to Thirteen.

I touch her face.

"Get off me." The words come out sounding more like a growl. I love it.

"Call me Lord, or I'll go back over to Fourteen and take my sweet, sweet time with her. It's been a while since I…"

I start to describe to Thirteen everything I want to do to that younger object. I tell her my deepest, darkest fantasies that I want to explore.

"Lord, please stop. Please. No. Don't…"

I smile. Now she's playing the game.

Instead of exploring my fantasies with the younger object, I explore them with Thirteen. I wish I could have this moment with Twelve, but she's not here. I'm going to be that monster that she expects me to be. Oh, she will totally enjoy the type of person I can become. I can't wait until she is mine again.

She will call me Lord. That moment will be perfect. I now know how I can ensure her cooperation.

Twelve

I have my first appointment with Ethan today. I don't think I have ever been so nervous in my life. I don't want to go. In fact, I am thinking of just not showing. Why would talking about something that I don't want to talk about help?

Unfortunately, my family knows me all too well. Victor and Maria show up at the house early in the day. I wonder why Maria isn't in school. I don't have a chance to ask. I wonder if she's okay. Victor wants to make sure that I have a way of getting to the appointment. He doesn't mind driving me since the therapist's office is right next to his school.

I start thinking: how am I going to pay for this? That is one thing that was not mentioned in the emails with Ethan. It never occurred to me to ask. I haven't worked in over a year. I went through my savings just to try to pay off the medical bills. I sold my car, my house. The only debt I have is medical bills and student loans, but I have zero income coming in.

If I wanted to be honest with myself, I wasn't actually planning on going to that appointment. Victor knew that.

"I can't go. I have no idea how to pay for it."

"Don't worry about it, sis…"

"I can't do this. I don't want anybody taking the bill for me. I'll go when—"

"So, you're going to lie to me, Aunt Mandy? You promised me that you would do whatever you could to get back to your old self. Is that not true? What other things have you lied to me about?" Maria asks.

"Is this why you are not in school?" I ask her. She nods.

"To answer your question, I'm not lying. See, in the adult world, money runs the world. I…I…I was just concerned about how I am going to pay for it since I have absolutely no income coming in."

"And Dad told you not to worry about it. So, don't worry about it. Since you're not worrying about it now, it means you're going, then, right?"

I nod. How can I not go? I promised Maria. I've never once lied to her. I'm not planning on starting.

I'm not even there yet, and I am overwhelmed. I actually take a shower, put on fresh clothes, and then am dragged out of the house, kicking and screaming. Metaphorically, of course. That's an exhausting, overwhelming day right there. It's only going to get worse.

I'm mad at Victor for bringing Maria. He knows that I can't lie to her. He knew that I would make whatever excuse not to show up to the appointment.

The three of us leave the house together, Maria taking the lead.

I look over at Victor.

"Is everybody in on this little conspiracy?"

"Yep. Even Meghan." He winks at me.

***

I don't know what I am expecting, but Ethan isn't it. He is understanding and seems to believe what I say without being patronizing. He seems empathetic but sincere. There is nothing fake about him, which I find weird. He even seems to have a sense of humor. He matches my sarcasm with sarcasm. What I find odd is that he isn't pushy. I have one hundred percent control of the session.

I also like how he has a Zen rake on the table. I put all my focus on that Zen rake, drawing pictures in the sand and then immediately erasing them. I just want to run away. I hate being there. It's overwhelming. He is focused on me and my well-being. It scares me. I don't know why, but it does. My last therapist spent all her time on her phone. She acted like she could care less. I'm looking for red flags with Ethan, but there are none. So, I spend my time playing with the Zen rake. It does seem to ease my anxiety some.

"Shall we schedule another appointment?" he asks at the end of the session.

For the longest time, I just play with that Zen rake. I have no idea how to answer that question. Yes, I want to schedule another appointment because of a promise I made. No, I don't want to schedule another appointment, because I am terrified to. My instincts are telling me to run. My instincts are always telling me to run and hide and to avoid contact with every single person. Ever since I met that monster, my instincts and judgment have been pretty skewed.

"We don't have to schedule another appointment if you don't want to, but if you change your mind, email me or call me."

"I don't know what I want. I'm just so afraid of everything."

"It's understandable, considering what happened to you. The fear is not going to go away overnight, but I think it will diminish some as we work together. You are not in this alone, and there are people out there who care about your well-being and want the best for you."

Against my better judgment, I schedule another appointment. I'm amazed; I feel a little better after that one lesson. I didn't think I would.

***

A girl in the neighborhood disappeared without a trace. She lived a couple blocks away. My parents and Meghan knew her in passing. The girl always walked her dog. Her name is Summer. Her disappearance was all over the news. I know who kidnapped her. It's him. I'm certain of it.

Later that day, I went to my session with Ethan. I told him about Summer's disappearance and how I feel guilty about it. I can't help but feel that it's my fault.

"Why does that make you feel guilty?" Ethan asks. "You have nothing to do with her disappearance."

"You're right, but I know who kidnapped her."

"Who is it?"

"It's him, the monster that had me. I'm certain of it. There are too many coincidences for it not to be the same person. I keep thinking he's around. I swear he's here. Now and again, I get a whiff of cologne, stale cigarettes, and gin.

Everybody keeps telling me I'm being paranoid, but he isn't done with me."

"I believe you," he said. "I think you are right, especially with him bugging your house and all. Did you know that girl is a friend of Jason's?"

I shook my head. I didn't know that.

"Have you told the police that you suspect it's that man?"

I didn't. I didn't think they would believe me.

I feel relieved. Ethan believes me. He isn't patronizing me either.

I'm convinced that the monster is always around me. At the same time, I'm convinced that my mind is playing tricks on me. I feel like I'm losing my mind. That's what the monster wants.

It's great hearing Ethan say he believes me. That gives me a boost of confidence. I am not losing my mind. That's what the monster wants: for me to question my sanity. The monster is doing his best to drive me insane.

After the session, I call Jason. I hadn't realized that he's friends with Summer. She is four years younger than he is. Together, we go to the police. The experience isn't as hideous as the last time I talked to them.

I feel a lot of resentment right now towards any police officer. With all their resources, they still don't know who this man is.

A couple of weeks later, I see on the news about a woman named Emily who was kidnapped eight years ago. Nobody knew what happened to her until now. The police just identified one of the bodies in the basement. The media was interviewing her family.

Ethan and I talk about this at our next session.

I knew Emily. I didn't "know her" know her. She was a victim of the monster. I didn't know her real name. I'd only known her as Seven.

He killed most of his victims within a week or two. Most of the time, it was faster than that. She'd lasted three weeks before she'd broken down and called him Lord. I had forgotten about that. The monster normally killed his victims after they called him Lord.

"That's why you survived."

"What?"

"You never called him Lord. You never gave him that satisfaction, which, I think, is the reason you are alive. The only difference between you and the other women is they all played his game. You did not."

"He kept journals," I tell Ethan. This is the first time I've really talked about what happened. He knows some of my story from the media and Jason. I could never talk about it myself.

"He couldn't break me. Even after the humiliation, the beatings, and the deprivation of food and drink, he couldn't break me. He tried different things. I just didn't want him to win. One of his tactics: he would tell me about his other victims. He would go into such intimate detail about them.

He would spend what felt like days just talking about one person. He kept journals on all of us, detailing every little, minute thing. He would read to me from these journals. They were awfully vivid. You have no idea. I did my best not to listen, but sometimes, the stories just seeped in."

"Honestly," I say, "I feel like I know the other victims. I can describe to you what all of them look like. With Seven—Emily, I mean—she had scars on her right arm from when she was in high school and a couple of bullies thought it would be funny to put out cigarettes on her."

Everything was in his journals. He didn't keep anything out of it. It makes my stomach churn just thinking about it.

I'm drawing designs in the sand with the Zen rake the entire time I am talking to Ethan. I can't bring myself to make eye contact. It's too humiliating.

"If the cops were able to identify at least one person, hopefully, they will be able to identify the others and catch this man. You have admirable qualities."

"What?" I ask in disbelief. Nothing about me is admirable or worthy.

"I'm serious, Mandy. You are an extremely strong, resilient person. You survived him when nobody else could. He's put you through unimaginable hell, both physically and psychologically, yet you are still able to laugh. I know you don't think so, but you do have an inner strength that's admirable. He hasn't broken you, and he won't. You are constantly defying him. Which might have saved you in the first place."

I don't see that about myself. When I look into the mirror, I see an empty shell, a broken human being. I see Humpty Dumpty. All the king's men and all the king's horses couldn't put Humpty together again. That is exactly how I feel.

It's weird talking to Ethan. I don't feel like a leaf being blown around by the wind, being trampled on. I'm still living in hell, but I'm starting to see a way out. Even with the man still out there, I am starting to see a way out.

Monster

I have three objects tied and gagged back at the house. Unfortunately, none of them are Twelve. I have Thirteen. She reminds me of Twelve in so many ways. She's a good substitute, but I can't wait for Twelve to be mine again.

There is Fourteen, the high schooler. She is associated with Twelve's family. I hoped she could answer all the questions I have about Twelve. She, too, reminds me of Twelve. She is a spitfire like Twelve. She spits in my face every time I'm near her. She does the exact opposite of what I tell her. Her whole demeanor is annoying as hell. I can't stand her. She claims that she doesn't possess any knowledge of Twelve. I don't believe her. I think she is being defiant and refusing to tell me what I want.

The third woman, I just met. She is not my type. I like my objects to be in their early to mid-twenties. This one is about ten years older than me. I met her at a restaurant. I was sitting at the bar, eating dinner. I was by myself and didn't want to be inconsiderate and take up space at a table.

I was thinking about Twelve and the others. I couldn't get to Twelve yet. The police had identified one of the bodies in John Smith's basement. That object had been from the same town that I'd taken Thirteen from. I hadn't thought it was. I normally don't strike in the same town twice.

 This is why I wish I had my notebooks. I'm slipping. I just need to let things cool over before acquiring Twelve. I was thinking about this when a woman came up to me and made small talk.

"Hey, do you want company? I hate eating alone," she said to me. Her hand touched my arm.

I accepted her invitation. We found a booth in the corner of the restaurant. It was quiet there. We were by ourselves. I didn't plan on taking her. It was a spur-of-the-moment thing. I really don't know why I did it. I wasn't thinking. It just happened.

I found that I was very angry towards her. The more she talked, the more I loathed her. She seemed like an evil person. She was telling me how she had two boys at home. Both of them were sick. They were puking, running fevers; it sounded like they were just miserable. Anyway, they'd been like that for two days. It was annoying her. She couldn't stand being home with them.

She'd asked a drunken friend to stay home with the boys for a few hours so she could be at a bar and grill with me. I thought that was horrible. She should have been home with her kids. She was doing all the talking. She wasn't letting me get a word in edgewise. I just nodded and said, "Hmm-mm," when it was appropriate.

"Do you want any dessert?" she asked me.

"No, I'm good. It was nice meeting you," I said as I reached into my wallet and grabbed a wad of cash to pay for both of our meals. I couldn't wait to get out of there.

She touched my hand. "The night is still young. Do you want to go back to your place or to a motel to have some adult fun?"

It pissed me off that she was out wanting to have some fun when she should have been home taking care of her kids. They were sick and needed her. She didn't seem to care about them, only about herself.

I accepted her invitation. I told her that if she really wanted to have some fun, we could go back to my place.

We walked out of the restaurant together.

"What car is yours?" she asked me.

"That one." I pointed toward a black SUV.

"I walked here. Can we drive back to your house together?"

We walked toward my car. I opened the passenger-side door. She slid in. I walked around to the driver's side, slid into the car, put the keys in the ignition, and drove off.

She willingly came with me, wanting to have some fun. Fun was what I was going to show her. I was nervous, though. I normally just keep one object at a time before acquiring another one. I've never had three all at once, but it is part of my plan. I need to prove to Twelve that I can become the person she wants me to be, that she needs me to be.

We got back to the house. The entire time, she was yapping. She didn't talk; she complained about this and that.

When we got back to the house, I asked her if she wanted anything to drink. She did. I slipped a little something into the wine and gave her the glass. After the wine, we went downstairs. She seemed aware of what was going on, but she couldn't participate at that time.

I tied her up. I took everything out of her pockets but kept her clothes on.

She is too old for my taste, but she can have fun watching me with the others.

I keep all of them drugged as much as possible. It makes it easier. I can't have anybody escaping. Or yelling so the neighbors hear. These are my objects. I need them.

Twelve wants them here. I'm sure of it. It's the only way I know of becoming that monster she wants me to be.

I go back out. I need Twelve. I watch her. She is starting to get her old life back. She is starting to go out more. She is starting to participate in life more. She's piqued my interest again. I want to spend as much time with her as possible. I don't want to miss a second of it.

Twice a week, Twelve goes to a therapist's office. It's right next door to the karate school her brother runs. They have a kid's class, an adult class, and a family class. She attends the family class with her niece and nephew. Once a week, she goes out with her parents, normally to a store. They're never gone for too long. The rest of the time, she is at home. Now and again, she is by herself. This pleases me. It shouldn't be too long until she is mine.

I can't wait until she is mine again. I think she will be pleased with what I have done. She will like this new game and the person I have become for her. I hope she finds it romantic. Everything is taking place at her old house. We just had so many great memories there. I hope we can create more.

Twelve

I find myself, for the first time ever, keeping a journal. I don't know why, but I actually feel inspired to write. It's better than talking about what happened. It's too embarrassing and degrading to speak it out loud. Truth is, I just want to forget. Ethan says I will never forget, but by talking about it or writing about it, it will lose power, and I will regain control. He also says I should talk or write as a way to help reintegrate back with myself. I really don't know how to describe my feelings. I feel dead inside. Where I should feel happiness, joy, and contentment, all I feel is numbness.

I don't know how to feel happiness or joy. Are they even real emotions or an illusion? I feel like I have weights tied to my body, and I've been thrown into the dark, cold ocean. I have no energy, and I really have to concentrate just to move. There is so much resistance fighting back. I feel like I have freezing-cold water running through my veins instead of blood. I no longer feel a warmth inside.

There is this invisible hand wrapped around my throat, squelching the life out of me. It holds me captive in the darkness. I cannot break free from its grip. It's too strong. I'm gasping for air, but there is none. I am trapped in this internal darkness. It doesn't have a future.

I really don't think I can do this anymore. I'm tired of feeling like a corpse, rotting, dead. I'm not living. I'm barely going through the motions. I am not eating. I am not sleeping. I have nothing but nightmares. I am not doing anything. Every day is a constant struggle, a constant battle.

I am hanging on by a single decaying thread. I don't want to continue like this anymore. I pray I will go to sleep and never wake. I am tired of feeling worthless, defiled, contaminated, and filthy. I can't handle this constant state of anxiety that I am in. I can't handle the constant panic and fear. I'm wasting everybody's time. I want to be dead. The only reason I haven't killed myself is that I don't want him to win. I can't allow him that satisfaction.

It sounds weird saying this, but I am slowly relearning how to live. I go to therapy sessions. Most days, I find myself looking forward to going to these appointments. It gets me out of the house and doing something. It helps break up the monotony of time.

That monotony is what's killing me.

I also started taking karate lessons. I wasn't planning on it. VJ loves it, and so does Maria. VJ wanted me to join. Victor has family classes. I wanted to see VJ more. At the same time, I was afraid to. I didn't mean to hit him. I don't think he even remembers.

I needed to prove to Maria that I'm doing everything in my power to get better. She wouldn't have anything to do with me unless I tried. Of course, Victor and Liz were giving me the spiel: It will help alleviate the stress, anxiety, and depression I am feeling. It will help keep me healthy physically and emotionally. And of course, there's the obvious reason: to learn how to defend myself. What sold me were the kids. VJ looked so happy at the prospect of me taking class with him. We don't see each other often anymore. I didn't want to disappoint him. And Maria once again reminded me of the promise that I'd made her: to do everything in my power to get back to my old self.

I have to admit, I do enjoy the classes. I'm starting to feel almost human. For the longest time, I was a nothing. I wasn't human, just an object. Even after I was found, I still felt like an object. I'm just now, over a year later, starting to feel slightly human. It's a weird feeling. Most days, I think of myself as Mandy and not Twelve. I think that's a huge, gigantic step for me.

It's also weird: I'm hanging out with Meghan more. We sit around the house playing board games and talking. Before the kidnapping, we could barely tolerate five minutes of each other. Something changed. I don't know what.

Meghan ran into my best friend, Randi. We've known each other since we were kids. I only spoke to her once after I was rescued. I just don't know what to say to people.

I can tell people are curious and want to ask me about the basement and how I am doing. They're not sure if they should ask. Sometimes, they hint around it. I pray that they don't ask. It's so uncomfortable. I end up not saying anything to anybody. It always feels like there is this huge elephant in the room that nobody wants to acknowledge.

"I ran into a couple of your old friends. Everybody was asking about you. They want to see you."

"Yeah, well…I don't want to see them. What did you tell them?"

"That we will meet up at a restaurant tomorrow for drinks."

"What? You have no right! I'm not sure if I want to go tomorrow."

"Come on, Mandy. It's just out to a restaurant for a drink. Some of your old friends want to see you. Randi does. I don't know why, with the way you've been treating her. She's concerned. Everybody is. Even me. So, I agree on your behalf. One quick drink, and if you want to leave, we'll leave. Come on, it's on me."

"Yeah, okay. Whatever, I'm not going to have any fun, though," I try saying with a straight face, but fail miserably. A part of me is glad that Meghan said I would go. I would have said no.

Since the kidnapping, I've always been compelled to push everyone out of my life. Friends, family, anybody, it doesn't matter who. It somehow became a self-defense mechanism, but it seems to cause more pain and more problems. I'm always isolating myself. I am so lonely, though. I just can't seem to forge or maintain any type of relationship right now. I do my best to sabotage them. Sometimes, I succeed, and sometimes, I fail miserably.

A part of me is upset that Meghan accepted the invitation on my behalf. She had no right to do so. I hate it when she does that.

The next day, when we leave, Meghan practically has to drag me out to the car. I do not want to go. I find myself easing up some on the drive. I'm not sure what we talk about, even if we talk. It seems like all we do is laugh. It still surprises me to discover that I still have the ability to laugh.

We made it to the eatery sooner than we thought we would. We are the first to arrive. We decide to grab a table instead of waiting around outside.

I don't like being in open spaces. It freaks me out. So many people can come after you from so many different directions. We grab a booth in the corner, away from everyone else. I seat myself so I can see the entire restaurant. My back is against a wall.

We are waiting. It feels like forever.

I get a text. The buzz scares me.

"Who is that from?" Meghan asks, bringing me back to the present day.

"Randi. They're running late. They'll be here in ten—fifteen minutes."

"Well, I really got to pee. I don't think I can hold it anymore. Wanna come to the bathroom with me?"

"Nah, I'll be fine here."

"Are you sure?"

I nod. "I'm fine," I say again, trying to put on a convincing smile.

I'm nervous as hell. I really don't want to meet up with my old gang. I don't know what to say to them. I am terrified of what they might say to me. I'm not in the mood to socialize with people. I'm tired of being alone, though.

Meghan leaves the table.

I pick up my cell phone and read some old text messages and emails. I'm just biding time, waiting for the rest of the party to arrive. The sooner they get here, the sooner I can leave. Ever since the basement, I've been feeling borderline agoraphobic. I'm totally engulfed in my phone when I get a whiff of that familiar smell: stale cigarettes, cologne, and gin.

I hear a cold voice. It sends chills down my spine.

I look up as I hear, "Twelve."

I look up at my assailant, paralyzed with fear. I can't move. I can't speak. He says something else. I can't hear him. I don't hear anything, not even the other patrons. I become very dizzy.

He shows me something. I don't know what. I find that I am even more terrified than before. I try to yell for help. I can't. I feel that invisible hand with its fingers wrapped tightly around my throat.

Monster

I need to acquire Twelve. The time has come. I can't stand it anymore. I need her. I can't live without her. I feel like I'm suffocating when I am not around her.

I made a mistake the first time I acquired Twelve. I knew she was going to be different than the rest. I knew she would be hard to break. I didn't realize how hard. I never really did break her.

That's going to change. I understand her better. I am not going to underestimate her this time.

My mistake with her was underestimating the power of her family. Her family has always been so close to one another. They seem to do everything together. I find it weird and, on some level, disturbing.

The way I figure it, I need her niece, Maria, as well. It's the only way. I think it's the only way of breaking her and controlling her. She will call me Lord. In the past, she has always refused to address me by my proper name.

But she won't any longer.

I just haven't given her the proper incentive. She can either call me Lord—for I am almighty and powerful—or she can watch what I will do to her young, sweet niece.

I follow Maria around for a couple of weeks. She always walks to a friend's house before trotting off to school. The friend lives two blocks away. Once at her friend's house, they walk to school together. Sometimes, they are given a ride, but most of the time, they walk. I can take her then. I wonder if her school is the type to notify parents when the kid is not in class. I wish I could find that out. I'm not sure how, though.

I wonder if the friend's parents would call Maria's parents if she were not there. I would. I wonder if Maria has a cell phone. I need to learn more about Maria and her friends. I need to collect her in the morning without causing suspicion or alarm and collect Twelve later on that day.

The timing has to be perfect.

I'm only doing this because of Twelve. I need her. She needs me to be that monster. She is always describing me to people as such. I don't want to disappoint her. I will become what she needs me to become. She is my oxygen. I can't function without her.

Only monsters go after kids. I never did, but this is what Twelve wants. She should really enjoy this game now. These are her rules I'm playing by. They're not mine.

I just hope she appreciates everything I have done for her. Everything I have sacrificed for her.

It's challenging following both Twelve and Maria around—as well as keeping three objects subdued in the basement. I keep them drugged most of the time.

Twelve's life is uneventful: therapist, karate, home. That's it for the most part. She only does that once or twice a week.

God, I miss Twelve. I need to see her. I long for her. I just want to hear her voice. I need to feel her touch once again. It's been a while.

She's at home. Only her sister is around. Everybody else is out of the house.

They are on the front porch.

I sneak around back, praying that the back door is not locked. It's my good fortune to discover that it isn't locked. The door leads to the kitchen, and next to the kitchen is the laundry room.

I get acquainted with the kitchen, laundry room, and living room. I've never been in here before. I'm looking for a place I can be where I can still hear the twins but where they can't see me. I am just about to step into the living room when the sisters come back inside. I hear the door creak open, and I hide. I can hear Twelve's voice. It's a wonderful sound. I just want her. I spend all my time thinking about her. I find myself getting all giddy at the sound of her voice.

I hide in the laundry room. Hopefully, they won't come into the kitchen. If they do, they shouldn't see me.

I can barely hear what the twins are talking about.

"I'm not sure if I want to go tomorrow."

"Come on, Mandy. It's just out to a restaurant for a drink. Some of your old friends want to see you. Everybody has been so worried. One quick drink, and if you want to leave, we'll leave."

"Yeah, okay. Whatever. I'm not going to have any fun, though."

There's laughter.

Oh, this is great. Tomorrow, she will be mine. She will see all the trouble that I went through for her. She will show me the proper respect that I deserve. I'm going to make sure of that. I can't wait. Tomorrow can't come fast enough.

***

The next morning, I am turning a corner at the same time as Maria. We collide right into each other. In that swift moment, I have my hand over her mouth. I am holding a rag with chloroform on it. In a matter of seconds, Maria passes out.

I pick her up and buckle her into the back of the car. I get into the driver's seat and head for home. That was easier than expected. I love it when things run smoothly.

I take her back to the house. She is starting to stir.

"Shhh, it's okay. I'm not going to hurt you. Drink this." I force her to drink some juice laced with sleeping pills. I check her pockets. She doesn't own a cell phone. I hoped a nine-year-old wouldn't, but you can never tell these days.

I take her down to the basement. I don't tie her up or anything. She isn't going to go anywhere. She will be too busy sleeping. I take out my cell phone and take a picture of her. She is going to be my leverage. Hopefully, the rest of the day will go just as smoothly. The others don't say anything or try to fight back. They either don't care or are too drugged to do anything. I keep all of them drugged. It's easier that way.

I drive to Twelve's parents' house. She is meeting up with a few people at a restaurant. I don't know which restaurant. I'm not sure of the time. All I know is it's an early lunch. I don't want to miss it for the world.

The house is at the end of the cul-de-sac. I wait on the side of the road. I've pulled over right before you need to turn to enter into the cul-de-sac. I put the blinkers on. I light up a cigarette. I'm reminiscing about Twelve. She has to be mine again. I can't stop thinking about her and about this moment.

Hopefully, once she is back in my possession, these obsessive thoughts will go away.

Twenty minutes later, I see her sister's car. I follow. I'm feeling a little bit anxious. It's been a long time. I'm not sure what to say to her when I meet up with her.

What if I can't get to Twelve today?

Or what if she doesn't remember me?

What if what I want to happen isn't diabolical enough for her? Thousands of questions race through my mind. I have never been like this before. I'm feeling nervous. I just need Twelve. I need her.

We get to the restaurant. There aren't too many cars in the parking lot. I'm not sure if that is a good thing or a bad thing. I watch as Twelve enters the building. She is more exquisite than I remembered. I have missed her. I can't wait to touch her again.

I wait fifteen minutes before entering the building. I notice her right away. She is at a booth in a corner. It's next to the fire exit. She is at a table with her twin. Her back is against the wall. A moment later, the sister walks away. Twelve is by herself. I walk over to her. I have the picture of her niece on my cell phone.

Twelve doesn't notice me approaching. She is too busy with her nose in her phone.

"Twelve."

She looks up at me. The fear in her eyes makes her look even more beautiful. I show her the picture of Maria.

"Do not scream or fight back, or this little girl will never see the light of day."

Twelve just gazes at the picture on the phone. She is unable to communicate in any way. I'm pleased with myself. I'm still able to surprise her.

"She's dead?" Twelve finally whimpers out.

"That, now, is entirely up to you. You do what I say, and she will be fine. You don't follow my commands, she will be dead. Come on. Come with."

I put my hand on her arm.

"Get off me!" she whispers.

"Fine. You will never see your niece alive again." I step back. I'm still looking at Twelve. I wonder what she is going to do. She sits there, looking catatonic. She doesn't yell out for help. She doesn't try to get away. I'm loving it.

"Come on. I've got you," I say reassuringly as I help Twelve out of the booth. I half carry, and half drag her out the fire exit. I hope nobody sees. I don't think so. Nobody is around. I find Twelve's cell phone. I throw it as far away from us as I can. I help Twelve get in the car.

Twelve

I wake up in a basement. My mind is foggy. I feel as if I have just woken up from a very bad dream. The basement looks and feels familiar. I'm horrified when I see a woman my age. She is naked but alive. She is covered in waste, blood, and bruises. She seems out of it, drifting in and out of consciousness.

I see another naked girl. She looks to be in high school. I'm pretty sure she's Summer, the girl who went missing. She's a friend of Jason's and lives in our neighborhood. She's naked, but I don't see any marks on her. She is tied up.

I see an older woman. She must be in her late forties. She has all of her clothes on, but she's tied like the other girl.

All three of them seem to be out of it. They're acting as if they have been drugged. In the corner, I see Maria. I find myself panicking. I'm calling and screaming her name, but she won't wake up. I want to run over to her. I need to check on her. I can't. I'm tied to a pole. I can't move. The more I struggle, the tighter the restraints become.

This is all too familiar. This is the type of restraint the man used. The more you struggle, the tighter and tighter the restraints become, cutting off circulation.

Shit, shit, shit. Fuck, fuck, fuck. Shit, shit, shit. Not again, not again. It's the only thing I can think of as the realization sinks in. How did I end up here? I can't remember. I was at a restaurant with Meghan. I can't remember anything else. I just can't remember. Is Meghan okay? How did Maria get here? How long has she been here?

No wonder everybody is naked. Clothes are reserved only for people and not objects to satisfy one's needs. Women are not people, only objects. Why didn't he remove the clothing from the older woman or from Maria?

"MARIA! MARIA! TALK TO ME, GIRL. MARIA!" I scream out. She isn't moving. Oh God, I hope she is not dead. I'm in panic mode.

The restraints are so tight, digging into my skin. I don't care.

"Maria!" I yell out again, trying to keep the fear and panic out of my voice.

"She's sleeping. It's okay. She's sleeping. She's sleeping. He hasn't done anything to her. Just gave her some pills. She's okay," I hear a voice say from the other side of the room. It's the woman who's about my age.

"He hasn't hurt her. He gave her some sleeping pills. He hasn't hurt her. He brought her here this morning. Who is she?"

"My niece."

We're here with him, the monster. I'm trying to regain my composure. I'm trying to wipe the tears off my face.

"Calm down. Breath. Calm down, Mandy. If he sees you like this, he will rape you again. You have to calm down, Mandy," I say to myself, trying to give myself a pep talk.

The man appears, seemingly out of thin air.

When I see him, I feel nothing but pure rage and hatred towards him. I don't feel afraid. I just want him dead.

"Hi, Twelve. It's been such a long time, hasn't it?"

He touches my face. I spit in his.

"Don't you ever fucking touch me again. I will kill you," I say to him through clenched teeth.

He laughs. My threat might have sounded more convincing if I weren't tied up, naked, in a basement. I do mean it. I'm through being afraid of him. If he touches Maria, I will make sure that his death is excruciatingly slow and painful.

"Do you know where you are?" he asks. His voice is so cold. It's devoid of any type of warmth and kindness. He's kneeling next to me. He is too close to me.

"Do you know where you are?" he repeats, brushing his lips against my ear. I look around the room. Suddenly, it occurs to me. This is my old house. We are in my old house, in my old neighborhood.

He watches me intently.

"Ahh, there it is," he says. "You do recognize this place. It's romantic, isn't it? This is where we first met. You came back here after your stint at the hospital. You invited me to your room. You would scream for me. Don't worry, I'll have you screaming for me again. This time, I'm going to make sure that you address me properly. You will call me Lord. I am tired of you treating me with such disrespect. I am Lord.

I am almighty and powerful. You will learn just how powerful I am."

He touches my face, my arm, my breasts. I don't like the way he's looking at me.

"It's been such a long time, hasn't it? I've been dreaming of this moment. I know you have too. We've always had a special connection." He stops touching me and stands up.

"Why are you doing this?"

"Because of you. Don't you see I am trying to be the person that you want me to be. You know, that monster that you kept insisting I am. You're going to love what I have planned for us. I know it. You were always so special. You deserve the best. This is it. I'm doing everything that you want me to do."

He walks over to Maria and caresses her cheek. He looks back at me, watching me closely for any type of reaction. He's laughing. He walks over to the stairs. Maria is still out of it.

"I'll be back shortly," he says. He laughs and ascends the steps.

"So, you are the famous Twelve? He calls me Thirteen. He took me because he said that I reminded him of you, and since he couldn't have you… The first time he raped me, he beat the shit out of me. I didn't feel like you, and he said that was my fault. You know where we are?"

"Yeah. It's my old house. He's made some modifications, though." I look around. It does appear different. "How long have you been here?"

"I don't know. A month, two maybe. I don't know. It feels like forever."

"You're Jason's sister?" Summer asks.

I don't say anything. Instead, I nod.

"He took me hoping that I could give him more information about you. You know, I'm friends with your brother and live a few blocks away from you."

"How…how did you get all those scars?" the older woman asks me.

"Him. He kidnapped me. He had me locked up in a basement for six weeks. While he…."

"Why does he call you Twelve?" Summer asks.

"Because I was the twelfth. He had eleven women before me. He tortured, raped, and eventually killed them."

"How did you escape?"

I hear moaning coming from the other side of the room. I look over. Maria is starting to move a little. She is the only one who is not tied up.

"MARIA! MARIA!" I call, hoping to arouse her. I don't want to yell too loudly because I don't want him to hear. The others start calling her name as well.

The man appears at the bottom of the steps. He looks happy.

"I hope you're enjoying this, Twelve. It took me a long time to come up with this. I desperately wanted to become that man you need me to be—the monster. Isn't it romantic? I hope you appreciate how difficult it was to orchestrate this. I did it all for you."

"What do you want?"

"I want you to make a choice." He walks over to Maria and pulls her up to her feet. He's holding her close. Way too close. It makes me sick.

"Do not touch her!" I scream at him as I fight against the restraints. Maria looks a bit disoriented. She's scared, but she doesn't panic. I see her touching her watch.

"I'll make you a deal," he says as he pushes Maria back to the floor. "I won't touch her. You have to choose." He points to Summer and Thirteen.

"Choose what? What are you going to do?"

He chuckles. "It's not what I'm going to do. It's what we are going to do."

"No. I'm not going to choose. Do what you want with me, but leave the others alone."

"Those are not the rules. You decide which one."

He grabs Maria again. She's whimpering. He kisses her on the forehead. Then he slowly touches her face. She instinctively swats his hand away. Then she freezes. The hand with the watch on it is pointing directly at the monster.

The woman he calls Thirteen gets my attention.

"Choose me," she mouths to me.

I shake my head.

"Choose me."

"No." Again, I shake my head.

I don't know what to do. He's going to hurt Maria if I don't choose. If I do choose somebody, he's going to do something much more diabolical to them.

"Stop! Pick me, just pick me," I say to him.

"You remember what we did together. Do you think she will enjoy it too?" Again, he touches Maria's face.

"Okay, okay, stop. She's only a little kid. Please."

He smiles. It makes him look even more sinister. I have to do my best to protect Maria. She's family. I don't want anything bad to happen to her. She's already in a bad situation. It doesn't need to be worse.

"Which one did you decide?"

"Her." I point over to Thirteen. "I'm sorry."

"Ahh, good choice. She reminds me so much of you. We are going to have fun, aren't we?"

He reaches behind his back and pulls out a gun. He instructs Maria to untie Thirteen and then me.

He tells us to go upstairs. He warns Maria that if she attempts to escape, or unties the others, then everyone will die a very long, painful, horrible death.

We do as we are told and go up the steps. He has his gun trained on us. This seems like it will be even more humiliating and degrading than what he did to me back in the basement. I never thought that was possible.

I can't believe he went after Maria. He did it so he could control me. My thoughts are on that kid. I hope she gets out of this alive. I hope it doesn't mess her up for the rest of her life. I hope she can recover from this.

I loathe him.

As we are ascending the steps, he tells me that I will call him by his proper name. He's right: I will call him Lord if I know that will protect Maria and the others.

The moment we enter the living room, both Thirteen and I start screaming and yelling for help. We came up with this plan without saying a word to each other. It might not work, but the opportunity is there.

After I was discharged from the hospital, I came back here. I remember my neighbors. All of a sudden, they had become very nosy and curious about everything and everyone. They wanted to know everybody's business regardless. I hope that trait is still there.

As we are screaming for help, I can't help but wonder why he hasn't shot us yet. It doesn't make sense. I start to wonder if the gun is actually real. It seems out of character for him, a gun; it's not as personal. I take a chance, and I go after him. We scuffle. He strikes me hard on the back of the head. I feel very dizzy and nauseous. I don't fall. I'm scuffling with him. I hope that it will give the other girl enough time to get out and get help.

I hear knocking at the door. So does the man. He tosses me to the side like a rag doll. The other girl is at the door. It's locked, and before she can unlock it, the man grabs her by the hair and yanks her back. He grabs her head and twists. I can hear her neck snap.

He curses as he leaves me alone and runs into the kitchen and out the back door. I'm feeling dazed. I'm not sure what's going on. He just disappeared.

The door opens up.

It's the police.

"Where did he go?"

I point to the kitchen. I feel very dizzy. All sound disappears. I feel like I am looking through a tunnel. I see a bunch of big, black spots. I pass out.

***

I wake up in the hospital. I have a concussion. People are looming over me. I can't make sense of the faces even though they all look familiar.

"Maria! Where's Maria?"

"I'm here." She's holding my hand. I cry. We both do.

"Where is he? The police have him, right?"

"No. We don't." There's an officer standing next to me. "We're looking for him. We will find him. We will find him. I'm going to need to get your statement as soon as you are up to it. We will find him, Mandy." The officer walks out of the room.

I don't know how he eluded the police again. I really don't. They were right there, less than a hundred feet away.

Physically, Maria is fine. He didn't touch her expect to get a rise out of me. She was walking to a friend's house earlier that day when he grabbed her. He drugged her right away. She was only in the basement for a few hours, and most of that time, she was asleep from the drugs he gave her.

He never touched Summer or the older woman. Her name is Kira. Summer was locked in the basement for one month. Kira a few days. The other woman was there for ten weeks. She died. I feel responsible for her death. I don't know what her name is. I don't want anybody telling me it. I don't think I can handle it, not right now.

Monster

We are ascending the stairs. So far, everything is going as planned. Twelve is going to do exactly what I want her to do because she doesn't want her niece hurt. This is exiting. We're going to have so much fun together.

We make it to the living room when both objects start yelling and screaming for help.

"Shut up, or I'll kill you!" I hiss at them. I shove the airsoft into the back of Thirteen's head. I know both objects hear me. For whatever reason, both defy me. Thirteen screams even louder for help. Twelve is looking at me weird.

Shit!

She calls my bluff and lunges at me. She's attacking me.

"Go get help!" she says to the other object as she is hitting me. She is doing everything in her power to subdue me.

Thirteen is going for the door. I hit Twelve a couple of times in the face. It stuns her. I go after Thirteen. Twelve is on me again. She is doing her best to hold me back. Even though I'm struggling with Twelve, I'm still able to grab Thirteen. I trip her. She falls to the ground, trying to crawl toward the door. She is about a foot away from the door when Twelve jumps on my back. She's gouging my eyes out with her fingers.

"Ahh, fucking bitch!"

I let go of Thirteen, and my hands instantly go up to my face. I grab Twelve's hands and pull them away. My eyes are burning. I'm having a hard time seeing.

Thirteen is at the door. She tries to open it, not realizing it's locked. I slam my back against the wall as hard as I possibly can. I can hear the wind being knocked out of Twelve. She lets go of me. I turn around and push her out of my way. I go to Thirteen. She's trying to unlock the door. I strike her in the back of the head. It stuns her. For a moment, she just stops.

I hear knocking and then "Police! Open up!" This jars Thirteen back. She no longer seems stunned, and she starts hollering for help. They have to hear her. There's no way they can't.

Fuck!

Thirteen is still screaming. Again, she fumbles around, trying to unlock the door. I punch her in the temple. I strike her at the base of her neck again. I catch her as she falls to the ground. She's stopped screaming. I snap her neck. I drop the body in the doorway.

I run into the kitchen when I hear the policemen entering the front of the house. I'm out the back door. I pray there are no cops there. There aren't any, and I am able to slip away.

I know all nooks and crannies of Twelve's yard and of that whole neighborhood. I had over a year to do my research, just in case. I'm hiding in one of those nooks. I figure it's safer than trying to get back to my apartment.

Fuck! What happened? Why are they there? How did they know to come here? I didn't make a mistake. There's no way! I don't make mistakes. I've been doing this for a long time now. I don't make mistakes. I'm better than that. Nobody saw me take Thirteen. She's been with me for a couple of months now. I am one hundred percent certain that nobody saw me take the other four objects.

I took away their phones just in case.

There is no way the police could have known.

I'm freaking out!

I'm trying not to. That's when mistakes are made. I just can't keep calm. Once again, Twelve had to go and mess everything up. I'm freaked. I don't know what to do. My plan backfired. I thought for sure it would work. Twelve and I are supposed to be together. Why can't she see that? Why does she have to ruin everything! We haven't had a chance to be together. I just wanted her to scream for me one more time.

She called me a murderer even though I've never hurt a man in my life. I just wanted to make Twelve into a monster as well, by making her choose who lives and who dies. She chose Thirteen. Now Thirteen is dead. I had nothing to do with that. Who cares anyway? She was only an object. Her death is all Twelve. She's going to insist I did it. I know she is. Of course, everybody is going to believe her.

How did they know? How? I need to know where I went wrong.

How did they connect me to all the disappearances? How did they connect me to Twelve's old house?

Okay, maybe a connection was made because of Summer. She did live in the same neighborhood as Twelve and is friends with her brother. And then, four weeks later, I took Twelve's niece. That is another connection, but I only had her for a couple of hours. Her family thought she was in school, and the school would think that she was sick. I am certain that nobody saw me take the kid. There was nobody on the street. All the blinds and curtains in all the houses were drawn shut.

Thirteen has been in my possession for months. That hag came back to the house with me willingly. She is the one that came up to me. There's no connection there.

I made sure nobody had cell phones, so they couldn't have been tracked that way. Maybe one of the neighbors saw that I was escorting women into the house. They are an annoying bunch with no sense of privacy.

All I know, it's Twelve's fault. She somehow summoned the police here. She always has to go and fuck everything up.

I am pissed off at Twelve. I put so much time and effort into making our homecoming perfect. She had to go and mess that up too.

She will call me Lord. I need her to.

I was right about one thing: the only way of controlling her is by controlling her family. I need to break her family one by one. Her family is what gives her hope.

They may not always get along or agree with each other, but that family gives each other strength. It's infuriatingly maddening.

I underestimated the power of family. That's why I lost. Fuck!

I don't keep any personal belongings at Twelve's house. When I bought the house, I didn't actually buy it. I was able to convince another person to give all his information. I paid him handsomely for it.

I eventually leave my hiding spot and go back to my apartment. I'm still trying my best not to freak out. For the first time that I can remember, I'm having a panic attack—or maybe it's a heart attack. I think it's panic. I can feel my world collapsing in on me.

I find myself pacing back and forth, back and forth. Everything is spinning out of control. I don't have my objects to help relieve the stress. I don't have the notebooks. I'm obsessing over Twelve. She is ruining my life, yet I can't stop thinking about her. I need her. God, do I ever. I've never felt like this before. I never knew an object could be so dense and obtuse!

I hate her for it, but I need her. She will become mine again. I am sure of it. I will break her. No matter how hard I tried to break her, I couldn't. I will, though. I have to. She's made my life hell. I should have gotten rid of her when I had the chance. I didn't. She is the only one I let go, all because she once called me a monster. I wanted—more like I needed—to show her what a real monster is, even if that meant becoming one.

I honestly didn't think that letting Twelve live would cause this much of a mess. I don't know how to clean it up.

Twelve

"Who are you?" I ask. I can only see the face. I can't see anything else; the rest of the body is hidden in darkness. I can just barely see an outline of the face. There is light reflecting from the eyes.

Cold, dead eyes.

The face slowly moves its way towards me, its cold eyes locking onto mine. I feel like I am in a trance. I can't move. I can't look away. I stand my ground, doing everything in my power not to panic.

It doesn't say anything. It slowly inches its way toward me.

"What do you want?" My voice trembles as it echoes along with the pounding of my heart. There is no other sound. It is dead silent.

"What do you want?" I ask again more feebly. The face continues to move closer and closer to me. Its eyes lock onto mine. I have the eerie feeling it wants me dead.

It cackles, making my blood run cold. I want to get the hell out of there. There is no place to go. I'm trapped in a room. It has no doors or windows. Nothing. I can't remember how or why I'm in the room. I just am. There is no way out.

The face is getting closer and closer to me. It's only about an inch away from mine. I can see it more clearly. I gasp. I can feel the rancid breath on my check. I can see into its eye sockets. Where there should be eyeballs are maggots. They crawl in and out of its nose and mouth as well. The rest of the face is nothing but bone and decaying flesh.

I recognize the face. I know who it belongs to.

"I'm sorry. I'm sorry," I say, my voice is shaky. Tears stream down my face. "I'm sorry. I'm sorry," I say in between sobs.

It tries to grab me. I jump back, hitting the wall. It cackles again, sounding evil.

"You did this to me!" it croaks out as it grabs me again.

I scream, thrashing around in bed, fighting my blankets. I quickly reach over to turn on the light. I'm shaking horribly. My clothes are plastered to my skin. It looks like I just took a shower with my clothes on. I'm sweating profusely. I'm shaking and feeling panicky and anxious. I'm feeling exhausted. I force myself to get out of bed. I'm afraid to fall back to sleep. The nightmares are so real. It really feels like I'm there.

These dreams have become more frequent and vivid ever since he kidnapped me for the second time. They have plagued me every night. They've even haunted me during my waking hours. I feel like I'm losing my mind. I'm barely sleeping. I'm no longer sure of what's real and what's not.

I'm always seeing her face, the woman he killed, in front of me. It's my fault she is dead. Ethan tries to convince me that it's not my fault, but it is. He killed her because of me. I called him a monster to his face. Because of that, he wanted to prove to me what a true monster really is. It's sickening. He made me choose, and I chose her.

I either dream about that woman or him and the basement.

He's still out there.

At least this time, the police have somewhat of an idea of who he is. They know what he looks like, his name. Well, maybe his name.

It's only a matter of time before he makes a mistake.

Maria saved us. I know she doesn't think so. She stayed calm under pressure. She has a smartwatch that has GPS in it. She can send messages, photos, and videos and play games on her watch. She sent a 911 text to her parents and had the video turned on, recording everything that the man was saying. There are a couple of frames where you can see his face.

The moment Victor and Liz received the text, they called the cops.

That's how they found us so quickly. It wasn't quick enough, though. A person died. I feel so bad for her. She was kidnapped and raped because she looked like me. If she did something that was out of character for me, he would beat her.

She was so close to being free.

He killed her in front of me. I did my best to stop him. My attempts were feeble and pathetic. I should have done something else. There must have been something else I could have done.

I do my best not to think like that. I can't help it. I go over that day again and again in my mind.

That man is horrible. It amazes me—all the cruel things he comes up with. I can't believe he was able to kidnap me a second time. It was even more humiliating than the first. That was so degrading, being there naked with the others. And in front of my family. He took our clothing. Clothing is reserved for people and not objects for satisfying one's needs. Women are objects, not people. Therefore, they should be treated as such. That is something he used to tell me all the time.

For whatever reason, Maria was allowed to keep her clothing. I guess she is only a kid and hasn't become an object yet. The older woman, Kira, was also allowed to keep her clothes. I don't know why.

I just hope Maria can recover. He had her for less than a day. She was drugged for most of it. Still. I don't like being around her anymore. I find it embarrassing. She's my niece. I wish that she hadn't seen me tied up and naked like that.

I feel bad I never learnt Thirteen's real name. I can easily find out, but I don't want to. I don't know. I just don't want to learn her name. I don't think I can handle it. I don't know. It's messed up. I keep dreaming about the monster, about my basement, about the others.

He killed her. He didn't have to.

He asked me to choose. I did. I don't know what he originally had planned. Something nefarious, I'm sure.

I find it kind of funny, but nobody believed me about the man. I knew he was still around. My family kept trying to convince me otherwise. I think it was extremely feasible, thinking that he was around me. He kept telling me how I was different from the other objects and how, because of that, he had something special planned for me. Meghan told me once that at least I am free. I don't think I am. I doubt I ever will be unless he is caught or is found dead.

He's a predator. He doesn't care who he hurts. All he cares about is sexual gratification, control, and violence. He plans his attacks, rehearses them over and over. Somehow, he is convinced that I am in love with him. In his mind, he doesn't think he has done anything wrong. I truly believe that.

That's what makes him so scary.

Ethan says he sounds like a very lonely, isolated person who lacks self-esteem yet feels very, very important. I think that's true. I don't know. He's just evil.

My family wants to move to a different corner of the country to get away from this monster. I don't think it would work. I think it would just piss him off and make him even angrier and more horrible.

I don't know what I'm supposed to do except somehow be more vigilant. I can't just hide in a corner indefinitely. I tried that all ready. It didn't work out too well. My niece, a high school girl, and two other people were kidnapped because of those actions. I feel responsible for it. I know I shouldn't, but I do.

Yet I really can't go out and live my life. He will find an opportunity and strike back. I know. He's succeeded in doing this already.

I just don't know what to do—or not to do, for that matter. I continue to go to my therapy appointments and to the Kenpo classes. That's about the only thing I continue doing.

The police are still looking for him. At least they know what he looks like now.

Six months have passed. No sign of the monster. I'm still convinced that he is biding his time. He still eludes the police.

I am so tempted to go out and look for the bastard myself. Something tells me I won't have to far to look. I wonder what possesses him to do what he does. He once told me how he hasn't killed anybody. He has killed twelve women, but in his eyes, it's not murder, because they were only women.

What happened to him to make him believe that only men are human and women are disposable objects?

I find that I talk about him a lot during therapy. It's embarrassing and humiliating to talk about myself and what happened to me. So, I talk about the monster. I can't help but wonder what happened to make him the way he is. Or was he already born evil? I have so many questions. It's weird, but I don't find him terrifying anymore. He's proven to be the spawn of the devil, but I'm no longer afraid of him. That didn't seem to get me anywhere. He just seems pathetic now.

He's still out there, probably obsessing about me. I find that I am fixated on him as well. I have a difficult time concentrating on anything else.

***

I never thought I would see Kira again, so I was surprised when I received a phone call from her inviting me to lunch. I am more amazed with myself for going willingly. I wonder why she wants to meet up with me. She was the older woman from the basement.

I haven't talked to her or seen her since that day.

My first meeting with Kira goes extremely well even though I feel really awkward around her. I really like her. She isn't anything like I imagined. I thought she would be broken like me, but she isn't. She is strong, and she just wants the monster to be off the streets.

The first day that we meet, we talk about the monster and our experiences with him.

"Hey, Mandy. Thanks for meeting with me. I hope you don't mind. I got your phone number off the internet."

"So, what's up?"

"I was just thinking about you and your niece. Hope you two are okay?"

I nod.

I'm not sure what to say.

224

"I don't know how you're dealing with this. I'm not. He didn't even really do anything to me. Not like you. You are all he ever talked about. What he did to you and the scars on your body. It makes me sick. I'm pretty sure I saw him the other day. It was at a store not too far from here. You seem to be handling it just fine."

"What was your connection with him? Everybody else was connected to me. Even Thirteen… God, I don't know her name. Why didn't I ask her what her name was?"

"Her name is—"

"No, don't tell me. I don't want to know. I don't think I can handle it. He killed her right in front of me. He kidnapped her because she reminded him of me."

She reaches across the table for my hand.

"Hey, none of this is your fault. It is not your fault. He is a sick, sick man. You asked me what my connection is. I have two kids. One was going through chemo, and the other had pneumonia. I was working over ten-hour days, seven days a week, trying to provide for my family. My husband worked from home. He was taking care of the kids. One day, he decided he no longer wanted to be a dad. He closed out our checking and savings accounts. He left me and the kids with absolutely nothing.

"I was just so hurt. I asked my friend to watch the kids. I wanted to go out. I went to some bar and grill and saw this man sitting by himself at the bar. He just looked so lonely, and I know I was."

"Why did he take you? Did he ever tell you his name?"

"He said I was a bad parent. My kids would be better off without me. I don't know what his name is. Honestly, I don't think I even asked."

"The police said his name was James Chantaz."

"Yeah, but then they found the real James Chantaz. Do you think he will take other women?"

"Absolutely! I believe he's going to come after me again."

"I believe it. What if he does?"

"I'll be ready. I want to kill that bastard."

"Have you heard anything more from the police?"

I shake my head. Honestly, I have lost faith in the police department.

"So, what have you been doing with your life."

"Nothing. I'm not living. I don't know how to. He's going to come back after me."

"Yeah, but you can't just idly wait around until he does."

"I know. When he let me go the first time, I shut down. I didn't do anything. For the longest time, I didn't go out, I didn't talk to anybody. I isolated myself from the rest of the world. Then he kidnapped, raped, and killed that girl. He kidnapped you, Summer, and Maria. All because of me."

"That's not true. You can't keep thinking that. He's going to continue until he's stopped. It's not going to be your fault. He's been doing this for a long time. He thinks he's invincible. He's going to make a mistake. He's going to get caught."

The conversation is quickly changing. I don't remember what we talk about, but it is nice.

After that day, we don't ever talk about him. Now we talk about life—or lack thereof. We talk about books, movies, whatever. Neither one of us brings up the monster.

I actually really like being around her. I enjoy her company. I always feel like I am walking on eggshells when I am around other people, but I don't feel that way with her. She doesn't expect anything from me, and she doesn't try to spare me from anything. She treats me like I am a regular person.

I always seem to have conflicting thoughts and emotions. I'm glad I am alive, but at the same time, I would gladly trade places with one of the eleven women abducted before me.

Before Kira, I was pushing everybody out of my life except my family. I tried to do the same with them, but they just pushed back. It was getting depressing not having that friend to hang out with or talk to. I wasn't going out. I wasn't working. I felt like an empty shell. I never thought I would be able to form a friendship or any type of relationship with another person. I felt too broken and filthy.

Kira baffles me. We've become good friends, and I've started going out again. It's weird—around her, I am somewhat able to live again. It's a long process. The monster is still around. I can feel his presence. I'm not going to let him defeat me. I survived the basement, and I can survive this. I'm glad we don't bring up that subject. That's something people seem to bring up with me even now. It's been over a year, and they still bring up the subject. Normally, they're wondering if the man has been caught. Still, it's nice not talking about him.

I'm going to survive this. I'm not going to let him win. I doubt I will survive the nightmares, though.

It's always the same dream. The room is pitch black. Someone is looming over me. I can smell the stench of death on her. There is light reflecting from her cold, dead eyes. I see maggots crawling in and out of her mouth and nose.

"You did this to me," she says.

All of a sudden, I feel so cold. I'm convinced I'm going to die.

"What do you want?" My voice trembles.

"What do you want?" I ask again as the person moves closer and closer to me. With her arms stretched out, she lets out a loud cackle.

"You!"

Everything changes. I'm in the basement. There are so many people here, watching. I can feel him in me. I can feel his lips exploring my body.

"I missed you," he says.

I can't get up. I can't move. I can't fight back.

As he finishes up, he wraps his hands around my throat.

I lie there, frozen in fear, my eyes tightly shut. He squeezes my throat. I am gasping for air. My lungs are on fire. He's going to kill me.

He's going to kill me.

He's finally going to kill me. He goes to snap my neck.

I jar myself awake, disoriented and paralyzed. It's only about sixty seconds that I can't move, but it's terrifying.

I do my best not to fall back to sleep. I see these images every time I close my eyes.

Monster

Things have cooled off. I guess I was just getting too cocky. It happens to the best of us. I was just wrapped up in this game with Twelve. She is the only one I let go, all because she once called me a monster. I wanted—more like I needed—to show her what a real monster is, even if that meant becoming one. It was so much fun, though. It was great being with her. She was better than anybody else. Her screams were intoxicating. She made me feel alive. I want to feel that way again. I need to make that happen again.

I am so caught up with Twelve. I've never felt this way with anybody else. I'm just trying to be the person that she wants me to be. She never seems satisfied, though. I think she's playing me, and that makes me so angry.

I wish I didn't need her, but I do. She consumes my every thought. I can't get her out my head. I try distracting myself, but nothing works. I would love to forget about Twelve and leave town, move across country, keep a low profile, and start over. But then it would feel like she's won the game. I can't let that happen. I never lose. Besides, she hasn't called me Lord. That has to change.

I need Twelve. I feel like I am suffocating without her. She is my lifeline. She makes me so angry, but all relationships are filled with obstacles, drama, and turmoil. I wish she could just appreciate everything that I have done for her and everything that I have sacrificed for her.

I feel so anxious without her. I need her.

I'm pacing around in my apartment. I'm not sure what to do. I haven't seen Twelve in months. I want to check on her, but I know can't. Things need to cool off a bit more.

It's hard for me to admit this, but I made a mistake.

My mistake was not killing Twelve. I could have. I should have. I let her get under my skin. I don't know why she was different from the others, but she was.

This mistake is costing me.

I no longer have John Smith's house, or Twelve's. I no longer have my notebooks or objects. The stress is too much to handle. She stresses me out even more. I'm not even sure if it's worth it, but she is my oxygen. I can't breathe without her.

I don't know why I became so fixated with her. Twelve is marvelous and exotic. The others were not. They were boring after a while. Twelve keeps me on my toes. She keeps me alive. It's exhilarating just being in her presence. Its infuriating being away from her.

I find it kind of exciting that she hasn't called me Lord yet. Everyone else has. I don't know why she can't or won't. She will. I'm going to make sure of that.

I don't know how to proceed from here. I'm good at my game. Before Twelve, I never made a mistake in it. This is a totally different game. I'm out of my element. That's what it is. I just need to find my stride.

I don't know how to do that. I'm not sure what my next move is. I've always been ahead of the police. Always. I'm not so sure now.

Right now, I feel like I'm a prisoner in my apartment. I guess I am. I am a wanted man. I'm sure the cops know what I look like by now. They know my alias. I can't even go to work. It's too risky. I'm stuck pacing back and forth, agonizing over Twelve.

I'm trapped. I have no place to go. I hate this feeling, so I decide to do something about it.

The time has come. I need Twelve. I feel like I'm going to die without her.

I decide to take refuge at Twelve's parents' house. Well, not at their house, but close enough. They live at the end of a cul-de-sac. Their property line is next to a state park. Behind their house is a nice, densely wooded area. That's where I'm going to stay.

At least from here, I can still watch Twelve. I can't badger her as much, though. I was going to destroy her family, one family member at a time. I think that is the only way to truly break Twelve, but I can no longer do that.

I have to come up with something else. I don't know what that is. I hope just watching her will be inspiring.

I am watching Twelve as much as I can. I need her. I need her to call me Lord. Everyone else has. I don't know why she hasn't. She is really irritating me. It seems like she is getting her old confidence back—slowly but it's coming back. She has even gone out a few times willingly. All that has to change.

It has to. It's not fair that she can roam around freely, and I cannot.

She needs to fear me again. She is nothing. I'm almighty and powerful. I am Lord. She needs to learn that. She has to.

I'm watching her. She is in her backyard, doing some yardwork, enjoying the sun. I'm relatively certain she is by herself. I saw her parents leave for work. I have not seen her siblings all day.

I can't see Twelve's face, only her profile, but she doesn't look afraid. She is acting like she is enjoying herself, enjoying life. This irks me because I'm trapped. I can't enjoy life. She took away all of my objects.

I hate seeing her moving around her backyard. She's acting like she doesn't remember our little game, and the hell she wanted me to put her through. How can she forget something like that so fast?

That's going to change.

It has to change.

This is the perfect opportunity to do something, but I am not sure what. I need to think of something horrific. I won't let her forget about me. I can't.

I can't stop thinking about her. These thoughts are driving me mad.

I want her to call me Lord. I need her to. She hasn't yet, and I can't let that continue. I already lost at my game, but I will be damned if I lose at hers. I can't let her win. I won't.

She is by herself, totally oblivious to her surroundings.

I leave my hiding spot and quietly walk toward her. My imagination wanders to all the things I can do to her. I have to break her to the point of no recovery.

She doesn't see me. I am about ten feet away, and she doesn't even notice me. This bothers me. It really does. I am letting her get under my skin, but I can't help it.

"Twelve," I say. She doesn't look at me. Maybe she didn't hear me.

I say her name even louder. I know she heard me this time. Yet she doesn't say anything.

She slowly turns around. I'm disappointed that I don't see any fear in her eyes. She isn't even making an effort to get away.

"You have mistaken me for something else," she says.

How can she act like this? We had so much fun together. All those romantic moments that we shared. It's disappointing that we weren't allowed much time together. We could be great together. I know she needs me as much as I need her. I don't want to waste any more time without her.

She acts like she has no idea who I am. She is not trying to get away. She is not yelling for help. There isn't even any trace of fear in her eyes.

"Have you forgotten about me?" I ask, shaking with anger. How can she act like this? She's pretending I'm a stranger.

People have always forgotten about me. Growing up, nobody could remember my name. It made it nice in school. It made it much easier to skip class. Nobody seemed to realize I existed. I thought I'd made an impact on her.

I thought for sure Twelve would remember me. I thought I'd made an everlasting impression on her.

"Twelve," I say again. I'm at a loss as to what to do. She is acting so differently. I don't like it.

"I told you that's not my name. I'm a person, damn it. I am not an object."

I do love her assertiveness. It's an attractive feature for her, but I don't like her attitude toward me.

"No, Twelve, you're an object. All women are. How many times have we been through this? It's time for you to come back with me. We had such great times, didn't we? I'm going to have you scream again. It's going to be great. Just like old times, but this time, you will call me Lord. You will treat me with the respect that I deserve."

"You know, Maria, my niece... You remember her, right? Shortly after the police showed, she was asking questions about you. About why you do what you do. Nobody could come up with an answer. After pondering about it for a moment, it occurred to her. You do what you do because you are a lonely, scared, pathetic boy pretending to be a man."

She's pissing me off. She knows it too. She will learn her place. I lunge at her, grabbing her arms and pulling her towards me. I expect her to fight back and resist. Instead, she steps willingly into me. I have a hard time keeping my grip.

She knees me in the groin. I immediately fall to the ground. She stomps on my stomach. The wind is knocked out of me. I expect her to run away. She doesn't. She stands a few feet away from me. She doesn't say or do anything.

"You fucking bitch! You're going to pay for that!" I scream at her. I feel so much hate towards her. She's such an ungrateful bitch. I did everything that she wanted me to. None of it matters to her.

I hope she runs. I love it when they try to run. I love that fear. I seem to feed off it.

She doesn't.

She grabs a shovel. It seems to have appeared out of thin air. She swings it at my head. I roll out of the way. She misses barely. She swings again and again, but she keeps missing. I'm back on my feet.

She holds the shovel like it's a baseball bat. I'm ready for her to take another swing. But she doesn't.

"You are so pathetic," she says. "Is that why you only come after women? It makes you feel potent?"

My blood is boiling. I've had enough small talk. She is going to regret all of this. I try to get the shovel from her. She steps out of the way and swings. The shovel hits me in the shoulder. I'm expecting it. I'm able to grab it, and I pull it towards me.

She doesn't pull the shovel away; instead, she thrusts it at me and let's go. I swing the shovel at her. She ducks and lunges at my legs, tackling me to the ground. I fall backward. She is on top of me. She punches me a couple of times in the face.

I'm able to grab her hands. We roll around. She is trying her best to get free. She spits in my face. I don't let go of her hands. I'm able to force her on her back. I'm straddling her.

Just like old times— almost. I just need to figure out how to get her to scream for me. Then it will be just like old times.

She is hitting me in the back with her knees. She is being such an ungrateful bitch. She can't even appreciate everything I have done for her. I've become the person, the monster she wanted me to be. It wasn't easy, but I did it. Just for her.

I'm able to hold both her hands over her head. She is flailing around desperately, like fish out of water, fighting to get free.

I'm loving this. I have her. My mind wanders to the possibilities I can have with her.

I hear a man's voice, yelling in the background. Instinctively, I turn to see where the noise is coming from. I see her older brother.

"Get the fuck off my sister!" he screams, pointing a gun at me. There's some distance between us.

Twelve bashes me hard with her elbow. I fall to the side. I'm only half straddling her now. I hit her in the face. I hear a gunshot. Pain sears through my shoulder.

I roll off Twelve.

She jumps quickly to her feet and starts kicking me and stomping on me. She has gone totally insane on me. I don't understand why. She wanted all of this.

Her brother is saying something to her. He pushes her to the side. He stands over me. He's pointing the gun at my head.

"You're never going to lay a hand on anybody in my family ever again."

He pulls the trigger.

Twelve

He's dead! I slew the beast. I'm actually not the one who killed him. My brother is. Victor shot the bastard. The monster made a mistake and touched one of his kids. Victor put several bullets in him. Everything seems surreal. That epic battle is finally over. I didn't think that would ever happen.

I can finally start rebuilding my life. I was trying to before, but it was difficult knowing that he was still out there. Still hunting for me. I keep expecting to see him. I know I won't. He's dead. I know for a fact that he's dead.

I thought I saw a shadow at the edge of my parents' property line. I knew it was the man. There was no doubt in my mind. I'm at the house. My parents were at work. Jason was gone. Meghan was asleep on the couch. I didn't wake her to let her know. It was my way of trying to protect her.

I didn't call the police. I really didn't think they would believe me. What was I going to tell them? That I saw a shadow. Every fiber in my being told me that it was that monster.

Instead, I send Victor a text: ***He's here.***

He sent me a reply, but I didn't read it.

I was standing on the porch, enjoying the sun. I saw a silhouette moving. I wanted the man dead. I was through hiding from him.

I left the porch, pretending that I didn't notice him. I had my back to him as I pretended to do some yard work. There was a shovel leaning up against a tree. Meghan must have forgotten to put it back.

The man saw me. I knew he had. For a moment, I could feel his eyes on me. He quickly disappeared behind some brush. I continued doing what I was doing, pretending I never saw him.

Minutes, maybe hours passed. I don't know. I smelled stale cigarettes, cologne, and gin. I tried my best not to tense. I didn't turn around. I heard his icy voice.

"Hi, Twelve." I didn't respond. My name isn't Twelve. It's Mandy. There was a pause that lasted an eternity.

"Twelve." He was closer to me. I was done playing his game.

"It's Mandy," I said as I turned around. "You have mistaken me for something else."

He looked stunned.

"Twelve, have you forgotten about me?" he asked.

"I told you that's not my name!"

At that moment, I wanted to kill him. He was a horrible, horrible person. He murdered twelve women. I remember being blinded by rage. I don't remember much. We were in a scuffle.

I kneed him in the groin. He immediately fell to the ground. I grabbed the shovel and swung as hard as I could at his head. I missed. I kept swinging, but somehow, the man kept dodging out of the way.

Somehow, we ended up rolling around on the ground, grappling. He punched me in the face. For a moment, I couldn't see. My eyes were watering up so bad. He hit me again and again. He was straddling me and had my hands above my head. I did whatever I could to get free. I spit in his face. I kneed him in the back. My escape attempts seemed futile, but I'm not going to let him win. Not this time. It ends here!

I heard a gunshot. The monster rolled off me.

Next thing I remember is hearing Victor's voice as he pulled me behind him. He was standing over the man, holding the gun to his head. He pulled the trigger.

Blood, brains, and skull fragments splattered all over.

Just like that, it was over. He was gone. He would never be able to hurt another person again.

I hear Victor. I think he's talking to me. I'm not listening to him. I'm unable to. I'm just relived it's over. It's finally over. I stumbled backwards, away from the body. I tripped and fell to the ground. I felt very dizzy and paralyzed. I couldn't move. I couldn't talk. Blood obscured my vision. I could taste it in my mouth. I thought he'd broken my nose.

I heard Victor on the phone. His voice was going in and out. I couldn't make sense of what he was saying. His voice sounded like it was coming from the other end of a tunnel. I passed out. I must have.

I woke up in the hospital.

I must have blacked out. I don't remember anything else. I vaguely remember being questioned by the police. It feels more like a dream.

They don't press charges. One of the officers seems disappointed that he wasn't the one to put a few rounds through the monster.

He destroyed so many lives. He killed so many women. He didn't think anything of it. It was a game, and women were only objects. I'm so glad that he's dead. I know so many people who feel the same way.

The man is dead. Victor saved my life. The man is dead. I can't process that information. He's been a huge part of my life for a long time. Now he is dead. I'm glad. That's the best news ever. However, I feel like there is a huge part of me missing. I feel so relieved, though. This huge weight has finally been lifted from my shoulders.

It's strange. The monster did everything in his power to break me. He wanted to destroy me piece by piece. He came close, but in doing so, he became overconfident and started obsessing over me. It took control of his life. Due to his fixation on me, he started to make mistakes. In the end, these mistakes cost him his life.

***

The six weeks I was missing had a major impact on my family. It's strange, but my disappearance gave my siblings direction. Jason and his band, the Free Spirits, started their own charity group: a shelter geared toward women and children who are victims of domestic abuse. Before theirs, no such shelter existed in the city we live in. Their charity has professional counselors on their staff, donating their time to help heal abused victims. They also help people find housing and jobs. They are doing their best to give abused victims a second chance at life.

It's sad to say, but that place gets a lot of business. The Free Spirits started it a year ago, and the shelter is going strong. Their charity has been mentioned numerous times in the news and magazines.

I am very proud of them. I remember when the Free Spirits first formed. All they wanted was fame and girls. They figured it would be an easy way to get laid. The band would try and get gigs. Sometimes, they would succeed, and sometimes not.

None of the members ever worked at actual paying jobs. They just bummed around, hoping for a break. They thought they deserved a break even though they'd never really done anything to earn it.

Jason and the members of his band now have focus, new drive, and goals in life. They seem so much happier. They are finally succeeding in their endeavors.

I am very proud of that band. I have known the members all my life. We grew up together, living on the same block. We all lived in our own utopic world, sheltered from the monstrosities of society by our parents and community.

When we were growing up, we would hear on the news about somebody getting killed or raped, and we would think nothing of it. It was like fiction. We saw such things all the time in movies, television shows, and video games.

Our parents, teachers, coaches, and neighbors, I now understand they were only trying to protect us from getting hurt, but in doing so, they also protected us from life. We never really understood about charity and helping others, even giving back to others. We grew up arrogant. It seems like most of my generation is that way.

I am glad that the Free Spirits are doing everything in their power to make the world a better place. My brother, my friends, and I now understand that monsters and evilness really exist. It's a shame how we had to learn that lesson.

Once a month, Victor and Liz give free two-hour self-defense seminars. These classes are geared towards high school- and college-aged girls. Not only do Victor and Liz teach the girls self-defense, but they also teach them to be aware of their surroundings, to follow their instincts—basically, to do everything that I did not.

I worry about them. They have changed since Maria's kidnapping. They are not quite as happy-go-lucky as they once were. They no longer let Maria and VJ out of their sight.

I hope Maria is okay. She seems to be doing well. I don't know what is going on with her, though. I don't think anybody really does. She is so quiet now. I hope that her kidnapping doesn't scar her for life. She is a resilient kid. I think she will be just fine. She goes to support groups. She actually enjoys going.

I honestly didn't know that they have support groups for kids. The one she goes to is geared for kids nine to twelve.

"Aunt Mandy, you should try the support groups again. It helps. Speaking at these groups slowly freed me of the shame I felt." The wisdom of a kid. Even at her young age, she wants to do whatever she can to make sure that this doesn't happen to anybody else ever. She has asked local law enforcement officers, her parents, teachers, just about everybody, what she can do to ensure the safety of other children.

I wish I had her drive. I dealt with these heinous crimes by shutting down. I couldn't function whatsoever.

Little VJ is a terror, like always. If he senses that somebody is sad, he will do whatever is in his power to make that person laugh. He doesn't like seeing another person sad.

Meghan and our parents teamed up with a small group of people. Everybody in this group has a loved one who was either kidnapped and/or killed. The group's logo is: "We find missing loved one's hand in hand with you so you are never alone in your search." This group brings awareness to the public of those missing; they support local law enforcement and families in all ways possible by using the media, the internet, and public awareness.

Before joining this group, Meghan dropped out of college. She said it was a waste of time and money. Fine, college isn't for everyone, but after, she always seemed to be in between jobs.

It annoyed our parents. They were paying all of her bills.

"I'm worth more than minimum wage. I am not going to slave at a minimum-wage job so I can be treated horribly," I once overheard Meghan saying to our parents when they threatened not to help her.

This group seems to be a calling. It was a major shock to her, but she really loves helping people. It's probably the first thing that she's ever stuck with. It takes a toll on her emotionally, but she finds the work gratifying. I never thought I'd hear myself say this, but I am proud of her.

My parents have a new goal in life: to make sure that no other parents have to go through what they went through. It's been a long road, but everybody in my family is happy. They all found ways to help the community. I'm so proud of them.

Meghan and I have a new respect for each other. I'm not sure when that happened. I actually like spending time with her. We have fun together. I never thought that possible. I think this is the first time in our entire lives that we actually get along. I'm really grateful for that.

The monster shattered my life, and I'm still struggling to pick up the pieces. He very nearly shattered the lives of my family, but they rose from the ashes. They were able to use an odious event and make it into something positive.

For me, it seems like time has stopped. Sure, it continued for everybody else, but not for me. Physically, yes, but emotionally, mentally, and spiritually, no; time has frozen. That specific moment has me trapped. Whenever I try to break free, it feels as if an invisible hand comes out of the darkness and wraps its fingers tightly around my throat and squeezes. My breath is forced out of my body. I can't break free. It only loosens its grip when I step back at that moment. It's funny how I can only survive by keeping myself in that moment. Somehow, survival no longer seems to be enough. That monster has made me afraid to live. He's dead, but I'm still terrified.

Even now, years later, everything is a reminder. Sight, sound, smell, feel. For the longest time, time stood still for me. Then, one day, it just accelerated, traveling at speeds faster than light. Years have been lost. It kills me. Right now, I feel like an apparition floating alone through the realms, searching.

I want the images to go away. I am tired of the nightmares that plague my dreams. I refuse medication. I'm afraid to try after last time. Instead, I have bought a dream catcher. It's hanging over my bed. It helps. For the most part, the nightmares have gone away.

I am just so tired.

I am tired of that invisible hand that is controlling me. It has me locked in that place. That hand is so powerful. I've been feeling it weakening, though. I hope that, one day, I can finally break free of that place. I do believe that, one day, I will be able to rise up from the ashes and make something of myself. It's a slow process, but I do think it's possible. His face is no longer sewn to the back of my eyelids. I do feel a small sense of peace. I still have nightmares about him, but his face isn't as prominent as what it once was. It's more like a blur. I can't make him out.

I no longer have nightmares about Thirteen. I was finally able to learn her real name. It was Sherry. It seemed that the nightmares about her stopped once I decided to learn her name.

I still feel guilty about her death, but I no longer blame myself for it.

I do continue with therapy. I find that I am starting to enjoy being around people again. I am no longer a video game designer. In fact, I used to despise that job. It was always a hobby. When I made it into a profession, I became resentful toward it, hating every moment of it. Never complained, though; I just did what was expected of me. I never really enjoyed life.

I wasn't able to pick up the pieces until I stopped trying to live that life and stopped trying desperately to get back to the way things were before the monster. I am no longer that person. For better or worse, I am no longer that person. Once I accepted that I would never have my old life back, I started to live.

I'm starting to enjoy life.

I will be able to recover from him. I'm not going to give him that satisfaction of destroying my life.